D1527650

Rise of
the
Giants

Other books by Christine Marshall

Charlie and the Giants series:

A Series of Retellings

Becoming Cinder

White as Snow

Forever Sleeping

Charlie's story

Rise of the Giants
Battle of the Giants
Last of the Giants

Rise of the Giants

Book Four in
Charlie and the Giants

Christine Marshall

To my adoring husband

Chapter 1

Am I *alive?*

Charlie's eyes came into focus little by little. Her body ached and water soaked her to the skin.

But I'm alive. Her shoulders sagged with relief.

The last thing she remembered was being under the water, lungs screaming for air, and a bright light blinding her before she passed out. Now she didn't know where she was or how she had ended up on dry ground.

It was then that she noticed the ground beneath her. It was rough, but squishy, and it trembled. It felt kind of like skin when she touched it with a tentative finger. She shivered. She scraped her wet light brown hair from her face, sat, and looked around. That's when she saw the enormous person in front of her.

The dark brown eyes of this huge person opened, tears leaving tracks in the grime that covered his cheeks. His face moved closer; his eyes studied her. His rough cropped dark brown hair sparkled with droplets of water.

Charlie scrambled back on her hands and feet and scuttled from a crab-like position to a defensive crouch. A scream escaped her throat. Her right hand reached for the dagger strapped beneath her dark linen trousers. She moved the dagger out in front of her, ready to ward off an attack. She looked back and forth between her big knife with its hand-carved handle, and what she faced. She didn't stand a chance.

Her hands shook. She was sure for the second time that day that she was about to die.

She jumped to her feet. A squelching sound escaped from her water-logged leather ankle boots. When the surface below moved, she saw that she stood on a huge hand. She stumbled as the giant moved to set her down. She did her best to keep her balance. The hand tilted and she tumbled onto the moist ground. The giant squatted and continued to watch her.

Charlie's mind raced as she spun in a circle. Fight or flight? She didn't know where she was. The leafy maples were at least three times taller than a normal cottonwood, their leaves the size of her torso. The coarse ferns that grew around the base of the trees were easily as tall as her, and the wide blades of grass came to her knees. What had she gotten herself into?

She faced the giant. Her stomach twisted. She was only the size of his hand. He was huge! His rough brown skin looked like earth. His chin was dotted with stubble which cast a shadow on his round face and strong jaw line. He wore a green tunic with a deep V underneath an open burlap vest and wood-round buttons. His almost-black trousers hung to his ankles. His oversized dirty feet were bare. He knelt on the ground in front of Charlie and stared right back at her.

"Hello." He drew out the word in his deep voice.

Charlie startled. Was he really trying to start a conversation? Was this a dream?

"What?!" she squeaked.

"Um… Hello?" the giant said again.

Charlie waited for him to say more, but he just crouched there like a crazy person. Her mouth hung open. Maybe she was the crazy person. How could the plants, trees, and this... person be so much larger than they were supposed to be? She pinched her arm hard to wake herself. It didn't work. She gulped.

"What has happened to me?" Charlie asked in a still-squeaky voice.

The creek beside her gurgled as the water flowed through the oversized grass into the enormous, dark forest. She followed the flow upstream with her eyes and tipped her head to examine the waterfall.

She thought the giant was tall, and he was really tall, but the waterfall was impossibly high. Her head spun. The water flowed from beneath the wall that surrounded her homeland. But she was on the wrong side. The humungous glacier boulders that made up the structure of the wall were stacked higher than she had known. Back at home, on her side, the wall was two times taller than her two-story house. Here, though, the wall was taller than the tallest too-big tree. She was a speck in comparison.

The pieces came together. Until a few weeks ago, she had never given the wall a second thought. It just protected her land and people from some unknown threat. Its huge glacier boulders towered over everything from home. Her house, the wood near where she lived, the farms and fields, and the little village with its town square at the center. It had no gate, no way in or out, just a wall that stretched on and on in a gentle circle. It had stood sentinel for over 500 years. Charlie was nearly that old, and she had never seen anyone come or go through, over, or otherwise.

But then she had started having this strange dream about trying to climb it. Every time, though, she would fall to the ground, waking just before impact. This continued for weeks before she finally asked her father what it could mean. At first, he had been reluctant to talk about it, but eventually admitted to her that she was a Dreamer. Her dreams were prophetic. He had been a Dreamer once, too.

Her father told her that the dreams were telling her she needed to go beyond the wall. For what purpose, he didn't know, but that the dreams wouldn't stop until she made it to the other side.

That was two weeks ago. This morning she had walked the path through the apple orchard and on to the creek that flowed under the wall. Since climbing was out of the question, she had thought to try to go under, instead. She had approached the edge of the fast-moving water, clutched her canvas bag to her chest, took a deep breath, and jumped.

Now here she was, at the bottom of an impossibly tall waterfall. Beside a giant. A. Giant. Not real. It couldn't be.

"I couldn't have survived a fall like that. There's no way," Charlie mumbled to herself. "This is just another dream. I'm in my bed having another stupid dream about the stupid wall. I knew this was a bad idea."

"Is something wrong?" the giant spoke in his gravelly voice which made her jump again.

She glared at him. "Yes, something is wrong. I know this is probably a dream. I'm ready to wake up. What's going on? Who are you, anyway?"

The giant looked taken aback. Why was he the one who looked so shocked at this situation? It was her dream. Right? This had to be a dream. She would wake up soon, and speak to her dad, and they would figure out what this all was supposed to mean. Right?

But if this was a dream, why hadn't she woken up yet? Why did this giant person still talk to her? What did it all mean?

Her heart dropped into her stomach. She was going to be sick.

This wasn't a dream.

All the crazy events of the morning had really happened. She had jumped into the rushing water and let it carry her beneath the wall. She had almost drowned. And then she awoke in the hand of a giant. Who was now trying to carry on a casual conversation while the tears dried on his very real face.

Charlie gasped for air. This new, oversized world pressed in on her. She plopped down onto the ground and tucked her head between her knees. The grass was soft. And big. It tickled her face.

Were giants even real? She had read about them in books about mythical creatures, but she hadn't ever considered the possibility that they existed. Clearly everything she thought she knew about her home, the wall, and the world beyond, was to be questioned.

"Who are you?" Charlie asked again. The queasiness in her stomach worsened. She needed to slow her racing mind.

"I am the guardian of the wall," he stated and sat up straighter.

"The guardian of the wall? I'm not dreaming, am I?" Her thoughts were still scattered.

"You are not dreaming. You have come as you should. And you will help me."

Charlie stared at him. What had he said? She was supposed to help him? Help him with *what*?

She stood and brushed the grass off her still wet trousers. "I'm not helping anyone with anything. I'm going to figure out a plan to get back home and forget that this ever happened. Where's my bag?"

She looked around for the bag that she had lost in the water high above. She stopped and faced the falls. The mist coated her face. She wiped the water from her eyes.

"How *did* I survive that fall, anyway?" she wondered out loud.

"The water. It keeps you young. It keeps you safe. And I keep the water safe. I am the guardian."

Charlie turned, eyes wide and mouth agape. "The water does what??"

Charlie had been a teenager for several hundred years. She knew that people outside her home aged much faster than she did, and wounds that only took seconds to heal on her own body would take ages elsewhere. She had understood that there was something special about life within the wall but had no idea it had anything to do with the water.

Learning more about this intrigued her. Yes. She would go home and ask her father about it. He must know something. He could tell her, she was sure.

She shook her head and resumed her search along the riverbank. She dug through the knee-high blades of grass for her missing pack.

She planned her return out loud. "If I make some rope, perhaps I can climb back up the cliff, over the wall, and back home… Oh! There it is." Her pack had washed up not far from where she stood.

"No, you will help me."

She turned to face the giant. He had risen to his full height, taller than the tallest trees back home, with fists on his hips.

"Is this a joke?" she countered. "I can't help you. If anything, you should be helping me get home." Her voice trembled. She turned her back to him so she could continue her search for something in her bag that would be useful for her return. She set aside her packet of dried meat and fruit, chunks of crusty bread that were now soggy, wooden hand-carved canteen wrapped in canvas, fire starters, sling and bag of stones. The thin, wool blanket that doubled as a shawl was at the bottom.

She sighed and stuffed everything back inside, except the bread mush which she left on the ground and cinched the straps. She sat back on her heals and surveyed her surroundings with an eye for any means of climbing back over the wall. But it was so tall.

She had already attempted to climb it on the other side, her home side, before, with no luck. How was she going to do it now?

A loud thud behind her shook the ground. She whipped around to see the giant on the ground, legs extended, crying. Again. This was insane.

She threw her hands in the air. "Why are you crying? What is going on?"

"You won't help me!" the giant choked out between sobs.

"Help you with what?" she shouted at the shaking figure before her.

"I have been waiting here for over two hundred years for the next guardian, and he didn't come. I don't know what to do. Something terrible has happened.

You are supposed to help me find out what is going on. And you said you won't."

Charlie pushed her hands through her damp hair, heaved another deep sigh, and looked at the giant as he sobbed. She felt bad for him. She really did. But she had no idea how she was supposed to help a giant with anything. "I'm sorry you're having a hard time, but I need to get back home. I'm sure someone else will come along and help you soon, don't worry."

She backed away from the giant, turned, and walked away from the creek and waterfall. She studied the wall as she picked her way through the too-tall patch of clover. Enormous glacier boulders, some bigger than her home, were stacked on top of each other, fitted just right so there was barely room for the mud-mixture that had been used to seal the stones together. Many of the boulders had moss growing on them. Some even had a tree poking out from the cracks, trunk bent in a U-shape as the tree grew toward the sky. Curtains of vines hung over huge sections, and ivy grew up other areas.

She tugged on some of the vines to test them. They snapped in her hands. Their roots were shallow and weak. Just like at home, the stones were too large and too smooth to even dare climbing. And the gaps between them were way too far apart to be of any use. Ugh. There had to be some way to get back. How would she pull this off?

She focused on the wall and thought of home. She strayed from the giant. Unconcerned by the distant rustling sound in the woods, she jumped when she heard a loud, vicious snarl too close behind her.

She whipped around and saw an enormous black beast break through the underbrush. The creature had thick, wiry hair that covered rippling muscles as it eased ever closer. It was taller than two bulls high, its paws padded on the ground with great precision, and its catlike eyes squinted as it sniffed the air between Charlie and itself. The ears were wolf-like, and it's almost-too-short tail swished. Enormous claws protruded from each toe, and the teeth that it bared were long. And sharp.

Charlie gulped, her palms slick as she grasped for her weapon. But her eyes didn't leave the beast. It paused momentarily, crouched down into a pre-pounce position, and its growl grew louder. She choked on the stench

coming off its body. She felt the growl deep inside her own chest. Her legs buckled beneath her. She collapsed onto the ground, dropped her dagger, and threw her trembling arms over her head.

For the third time that day, she was sure she about to die.

Chapter 2

The snarling cut off. The pain never came. She was still in one piece. She looked up and saw the creature's head on the ground, separated from its body. Blood pulsed out into a pool. The giant stood behind the beast's body; a bloody sword dangled from one hand.

"What was that thing?" Charlie panted as she stood.

"That dark creature is attracted to giants. There will be more. You are supposed to help me."

Charlie's eyes widened. "Dark creature? Does it have dark magic or something?"

The giant shrugged. "I call it a dark creature because, well… because it's dark." The corners of his mouth twitched.

Charlie shook her head. What was going on out here? She was glad the giant had saved her life and everything, but, still, she had no clue what she was supposed to do.

A mythical giant stood before her. A mysterious creature lay dead on the ground. And questions about the life-prolonging water tickled the back of her mind. The urgency to return home was being replaced by curiosity about the world in which she had fallen.

She glanced at the giant, afraid to set off his tears again, and asked, "Why do you keep saying that I'm supposed to help you? I can't see how I could possibly help you from a thing like that." She pointed at the dead creature and shuddered.

The giant wiped his sword on the moss of a nearby tree three times larger than it should be, and replaced it in the sheath strapped to his waist. He leaned against a different tree and sunk to the ground. The tree groaned against his weight. He took several deep breaths. It seemed like talking took a great deal of effort for this oversized man. Her curiosity blossomed.

The giant spoke once more. "I know you are a Dreamer."

Charlie's jaw dropped. "What…. How do you…"

The giant raised his hand, silently telling her to let him explain. "I know you are a Dreamer. I know you dreamt about leaving the wall and coming to the other side. I, too, had a dream. About you." He bent his head down and looked Charlie straight in the eye and said, "and you *are* supposed to help me."

Charlie staggered to a moss-covered rock nearby and angled herself so she couldn't see the hideous dead animal. She sunk down. As if everything else that had happened lately wasn't strange enough.

She had been surprised to learn that her father was also a Dreamer. Charlie understood that it was normal for people to dream. She had dreamt her entire life. But when she started to have dreams about the wall, her dreams had changed. They had become much more vivid, every sense enhanced as she had climbed and fallen from the wall over and over again in her dreams. They had been different. That's what her father had meant by saying they were "Dreamers." And now the giant said he was one, too.

"This changes… everything." She looked at the dark creature over her shoulder. "I need a few minutes to think. Do you mind sitting here with me?" She hugged herself and thought about what would happen if one of those creatures found them again. Or what might the giant do if she abandoned her dreams and returned home.

The giant let out a low chuckle. "No, I don't mind. If I'm good at anything, it is waiting." His head tipped back and rested against the tree, and he closed his eyes.

Charlie's head spun. She focused on taking even, steady breaths and relaxed her whole body.

She could see herself in the water going under the wall. The current had started out gentle, and she was relaxed as she floated on the surface. The current changed. It sped up and tossed Charlie around. She spluttered and squeezed her eyes shut. Her left arm smashed into an unseen rock, and she cried out in surprise even as she felt her arm begin to heal. Soon water gurgled and splashed all around her. She lost all sense of direction. She tried her best to catch her breath but was repeatedly dragged below the surface. She clung tighter to her pack. She couldn't see anything. Scrapes and gashes cut open her skin along her arms and face. She ignored the pain as each new cut healed in a heartbeat. She focused on keeping her head above the water. The channel shrunk. Before long the gap between the water and the roof vanished. The straps of her pack slipped off her shoulders and it was tugged away from her. She held her breath for as long as possible. Her eyes stung in the dark water. Her lungs burned with the fluid that was in them. It took all her effort to not breathe. The river hurried her along. She couldn't hold her breath for much longer. Each second felt like an eternity. The bright sunlight blinded her from the other side of the tunnel. She lost consciousness.

She saw herself fall on this side of the wall, which was crazy, because she had been unconscious. It was unsettling seeing her limp form fall from such a height, arms and legs flailing. She watched as the giant caught her with his massive hands. He had a look of expectation on his face as he peered at the diminutive Charlie.

She tried to think of home, her father, but the thoughts wouldn't materialize. It was as if the home she had left behind was hidden in a thick fog that Charlie's mind couldn't penetrate.

When she thought of the giant again, his form was clear in her mind.

A sensation of calm overwhelmed Charlie. She was right where she was supposed to be. There was something important she was supposed to do. For the first time in weeks her mind wasn't consumed with thoughts of crossing over the wall, one direction or the other.

Charlie opened her eyes and refocused on her strange surroundings. The too-big grass was thick and lush. Patches of purple foxgloves and morning glories spotted the ground, each blossom the size of her hand. Even the pine needles were longer and thicker than she had previously seen. When her gaze landed on the giant, it hit her with great force: she believed she was meant to help him. The only thing left to do was to figure out how.

She studied the giant as he struggled to keep his head from dropping to his chest. It looked like he probably cut his own hair. How fast did it grow? How fast did *he* grow? The bottoms of his feet were thick with calluses, but she noticed that a pair of hand-stitched leather moccasins dangled from his belted pants on one side. So, he chose not to wear shoes. Why? He had said he had been waiting for… what was it… two hundred years or something? How old was he? Before she realized she was saying it, the words "I will help you," spilled from her mouth in a sort of holler.

He startled and his eyes flew open. He rubbed his hands over his tired face and let out a sigh of relief.

"What is it you need me to do?" Charlie asked him.

The giant looked down at her. Then he inspected his hands. Then his eyes moved to his legs and feet. Then at the tree next to her, then the sky. "Well…. That's the thing. I…. don't know."

"That does complicate things, doesn't it?" Charlie sighed as she stood and shouldered her pack.

"Yes…" the giant answered.

"When you saw me in your dream, what did you see me do?" She would puzzle this out, one way or another.

"Nothing. I just saw you, Charlie."

Charlie jumped. "How do you know my name??"

"I told you. I saw you in a dream. I know, Charlie." His expression was warm.

Even though she started to feel flustered again, she stayed calm. "If I had a dream to get over the wall, and you had a dream about me coming, then maybe what we need is another dream to help us figure out what to do next."

"That sounds right." The giant nodded.

Chapter 3

"There will be more beasts. We should move. It will be harder for them to track me." The giant stood.

"Wonderful." The last thing she wanted was to see one of those again.

"And I know whatever it is we must do; it is not here." The giant concluded.

"Where do we go?" Charlie wanted to know.

The giant brought his face low. He looked Charlie right in the eyes. It was like he could see inside her or something. She took a half a step back.

"Charlie, I am not sure where we should go. But I think we should begin by moving away from the wall."

Charlie nodded. She took a deep breath. "Great, you lead the way." What was she doing out here anyway? The doubt creeped back. She pushed it away, lifted her chin, and followed the giant.

The giant stretched to his full height and took a course perpendicular to the wall. Charlie followed him through the forest. The air was heavy with humidity and sweet and spicy with the smell of stargazer lilies. Moss dangled from the mixture of spruce and deciduous trees and the ground was soft under Charlie's feet. The trees were about twice as tall as the giant. The bright coneflower blossoms scattered on the forest floor were as wide as Charlie's arm span, and the button mushrooms that grew here and there were the size of large pumpkins. The giant was the right size in proportion to their surroundings. Charlie was small. So small. She focused on following the giant.

For each of the giant's long strides, Charlie had to jog at least a dozen steps. He would take two or three steps and stop to wait for her to catch up. Before long, her pace slowed, and after a while, she stopped. The giant took a couple of steps back to her and asked what was the matter.

"Just tired. I don't think I can keep up. We'll never get anywhere at this pace."

"Would you like me to carry you?"

"Carry me?" she choked on the words.

"Yes, here on my shoulder." The giant reached down and placed his hand on the ground, palm up.

When he lifted her, she squatted to maintain her balance. He tipped her onto his shoulder where she scrambled into a sitting position. She gripped the edge of his vest with both hands.

"Comfortable?" the giant asked.

"Sure, I guess." Her knuckles turned white as she clung to his vest.

At first it was unsettling being up so high on something that moved. After a little while, though, she loosened her grip.

They didn't talk at first, and it didn't bother her. Her father was a thoughtful person, always planning inventions, and he seldom shared his thoughts out loud. She had inherited this from him, spending her own time reading or sketching when she was at home.

Charlie's curiosity about the giant won out after several hours, though. "So," she said to him, finding it much easier to talk to him from his shoulder than the ground. "How tall are you, anyway?"

"Tall enough."

Charlie chuckled.

"What?" the giant blushed. "I'm short for my age."

Was he self-conscious about his height? Charlie grinned. "That's fine, I'm almost five hundred years old. I'm a little short for my age, too. Don't you think?"

The giant's cheeks returned to their normal color.

"So, why are all the plants and trees out here so big?" Charlie changed the subject. "Where I live, everything is so much smaller."

"I hadn't realized the plants are not this size on your side of the wall." The giant looked thoughtful.

"Nope. But what makes them so big out here? I mean, is the whole rest of the world like this?" It was intimidating to think about, being so small in a world where everything was so oversized. Did she belong? Was it safe?

"The water makes everything larger than usual. And it's not all like this, you'll see."

They walked along the river Charlie had emerged from and followed it as it meandered away from the wall and Charlie's home.

"How does the water do that?" Charlie wanted to know.

"The water that flows within the wall comes from the Deep Spring that originates deep underground, near the center of our world. The minerals in the water are imbued with an old magic that extends life and heals. It also protects the plants along its path and allows them to grow faster and stay healthier."

"So how come the plants and trees on my side of the wall aren't as big?"

The giant hesitated. "The enchantments that protect your home negate the effects of the water within the wall. On everything except the people. There were special protections put into place when the wall was built. People out here do not live as long as you."

Charlie nodded. "The shortened memories?" There might be a connection. Her father had always evaded questions about this topic. And the library had been useless. She learned to live with the fact that her questions may not have answers.

The giant glanced sideways at Charlie. "Yes, the shortened memories."

Charlie pondered this information. Back home, people had long lives, yes. But they also had short memories. The people remembered things for only about a year. After that the memories faded. Most of them were unaware of their memory loss. They retained instincts for survival, sense memories, and feelings towards other people. But they didn't remember any details about their life prior to the previous year.

Charlie and her father were the only ones who retained their memories. Charlie carried the memories of the last several hundred years with her. Every book she had read. Every skill she had learned. Every dream, conversation, and relationship she experienced.

Over time the memories grew heavy. Charlie had gone through phases when she wished she would forget. It was hard being the only child, and later the only teenager, who could remember the quarrels and the fun of the previous year. The other people from her home were happy, but they also seemed to be missing out on so much of life. This is what had led Charlie to be grateful for her retained memories, though she had never understood why she and her father were unique.

How could there be so much that she hadn't known about her home? About the world? Slowly a few thoughts settled together. "Is that why you guard the wall? To protect the Deep Spring?"

"Yes. To protect the Deep Spring. You can imagine what that kind of healing and life sustaining power could do in the wrong hands."

Charlie nodded. "So, that must be why the wall is there, too?"

She had never been able to get much information about the wall, other than it was put in place to protect its inhabitants.

"Yes. The wall is there to protect the Deep Spring, and the giants stand guard to protect the wall."

"I've never heard of anyone coming inside the wall. Is there a real danger of that happening?"

The giant looked at Charlie sideways. He hesitated again and let out a faint sigh. "Yes. There is." He had the demeanor of someone defeated.

Charlie gasped. "Did you ever have to fight anyone off? From the wall, I mean. Did you have to defend it?" Her hand moved to her chest at the thought of she and her people coming close to destruction without knowing anything about the outside world.

"Well… no," replied the giant.

Charlie drew her eyebrows together. "But you said the danger was real. If you've never seen anyone come to attack the wall, then how do you know?"

The giant cleared his throat. "The truth is, I didn't exactly stay at my post the entire time."

"What? You didn't? Why not? What happened??"

"It's a long story."

Charlie laughed. "Well, get started! I have time!"

Chapter 4

The pair found a clearing in the trees, and the giant wiped away some laurel bushes with one of his large hands before he lowered Charlie to the ground. The upturned earth was soft and aromatic with decaying leaves and broken pine needles. Now the giant could tell his story, they could share a meal… what did giants eat, anyway? And hopefully find some sleep.

The sun dipped towards the horizon. Charlie spread out her still damp things from her pack on a warm boulder to dry. She hung her wool blanket on a tree branch nearby to let the last of the water evaporate away in the dying sunlight. After she gathered twigs and stones, along with a couple of dried branches, Charlie started a fire. She had anticipated the wetness of the river and had wrapped the fire-starting supplies in several layers of animal hide.

As Charlie prepared for the evening she asked the giant, "So, tell me about the time you left the wall."

The giant lowered himself against one of the massive oak trees at the edge of the clearing and told Charlie his story.

"After one hundred years my replacement was supposed to come so I could find a place to sleep. It is difficult for us to stay awake for so long. He didn't come. After another twenty years had passed, I knew something must be wrong.

"We are a patient race, so I decided to wait longer, thinking that maybe my replacement had overslept. After fifteen more years I couldn't take it anymore. I spent a couple of years debating whether I should leave the wall."

"A couple of years debating? Why not just leave right away?" Charlie interrupted in between breaths as she blew on the fire.

"Because I knew that if my replacement hadn't come by then, something must be wrong. Would I be leaving my post to danger? But how could I know what was wrong if I stayed?

"So, after thinking about it for two years, I decided to find out what was going on. I traveled through valleys and over mountains. It took me six whole days until I saw something in the distance that seemed off. When I got closer, I could smell the forest burning and hear the sound of thousands of human voices. I stayed hidden behind some boulders a man's-half-day-journey from the commotion. What I saw terrified me."

The giant paused. Charlie stopped adding wood to the now bright fire and glanced at him. She waited for him to continue.

"There was a sleeping giant in the midst of thousands of armor-clad men and dozens of those dark creatures you encountered before. They had nearly finished constructing something over him. I was confused, but frozen with fear. I had no choice but to watch.

"After several hours they finished their contraption. It was built around the sleeping giant's chest. It had a counterweight at one end and a huge blade that hung over the giant. At the precise moment I realized what they were about to do, the humans shouted and cut a rope holding the counterweight. The blade dropped and plunged right into the giant's chest. I couldn't believe my eyes. I had witnessed the murder of a giant."

"What did you do?" Charlie cried.

"I knew I must flee. The dark creatures were sniffing the air. Fear forced me to rush back to my post, arriving in just a day and a half, afraid for my own life and for the future of other sleeping giants. We are near impossible to kill when we are sleeping. Our skin grows hard, rocklike. But somehow these men have found a way to slay us during our slumber."

The giant's breath was heavy by the time he was finished. It must have been difficult for him to relive this.

She placed a hand on his leg. "I am so sorry. That must have been awful. What do you think it means? What could be their motive?"

"I'm not quite done with my story. I will finish now.

"When I returned to my guard post, I was worried about what I had just seen. I had no idea what was going on while I was on duty. I didn't have any trouble staying awake for many years after that. Several times since my return, those dark creatures have arrived, but each time I was able to kill them.

"Then about fifty years ago, I slept for a while and had a dream. I dreamt about a person coming out from the falls and helping me defeat this mysterious enemy. I saw many things in my dream. But most important of all, Charlie, I saw you."

He spoke in a soft voice, "I'm not sure what we are supposed to do. But I know you can help."

"I will help you. Whatever it takes." She felt deep down inside that she would be able to help.

She moved back to the fire and to her things spread out to dry. She would stay by his side and do anything in her power to help him figure out who was behind slaying the giants. Maybe intentionally seeking out evil was a bad idea, like marching toward her own death, but she knew she would be safe with the giant by her side.

She picked up the things from her pack that had finished drying, and was about to load it all back in. As she opened her pack to drop in the first bundle of tools, she saw something she hadn't noticed before hidden in the shadows at the bottom of her bag. She knew she hadn't put it there and had no idea where it came from.

She pulled out a bundle wrapped in several layers of leather and inspected it. She couldn't remember if she had seen it before. Nothing came to mind, so she opened it. Inside she found some damp parchment wrapped around a vial that had a leather cord attached to it. She set the pouch and vial in her lap and opened the paper.

It was a letter from her father. Her heart leapt into her throat. She swallowed hard and opened the letter.

> *My Little Charlie,*
> *I know you will be surprised to receive a letter from me, and I know you will find it before the time comes that you will need it. I have enclosed a vial of the Deep Spring water. Keep it safe, as it will be a valuable asset to you on your journey. The giant should have explained the significance of the water by now.*

Charlie whipped her head to look at the giant. How had her dad known about the giant? Had he had a dream, too? What had it told him? Why hadn't he shared it with her?

Her eyes returned to the paper in her hands.

Charlie, I have seen your journey in a dream. I know what you are capable of, and I know you have a good heart. Keep your friends close and pay attention to all your dreams while you travel. They will tell you the things you should do.

That explained it, at least a little.

What you, the giant, and others you will meet on your way are about to accomplish is bigger than me, you, or our home. It is for the future of the entire world. You have been chosen for a reason. Make good choices and you will do great things; more than you think you are capable of.
I am sorry that I have not spoken with you about this already. It is hard for me to let go of you after losing your mother. She would have been proud of the decision you have made.

Charlie swallowed another lump in her throat.

I have seen more of your journey than I can tell you now. You must discover the path for yourself in order for you to accomplish your goals. The woman you become will be a result of your experiences.
Always remember who you are and that I love you.

A couple of fat tears dripped onto the parchment. She couldn't take her eyes off it. She skimmed each paragraph a few more times. It was crazy that he knew about the giant. And what about the other friends she would make on her journey? If only she could talk to him, ask him these questions and get answers right away.

But that was not to be. She folded the letter and tucked it back into the leather pouch. She allowed his words to bring her comfort and courage. Next, she picked up the vial and held it close to her eyes. The water within sparkled in the firelight. What had her father seen in his dream and what would she need it for?

Charlie kept these thoughts to herself as she settled near the fire to stay warm in the darkness. She nibbled on some of the dried meat she had brought along and drank water from her canteen. She savored the sweetness on her tongue. She watched the fire dance as her eyes grew heavy. Before long, she was asleep.

That night Charlie had two dreams.

In the first she dreamt of a beautiful meadow with orange butterfly-weeds, pink queen-of-the-prairies, bright yellow goldsturms, violet geraniums, white angelicas and a rainbow of lupines. Iridescent butterflies of blues and reds floated on the breeze, and a mother deer with her fawn grazed in the tall emerald grass. Deciduous oaks, maples, and rowan trees surrounded the meadow and their full leaves whispered in the breeze. The bright sun gave everything a warm glow. The sun felt so good on her skin and warmed her as she sunk onto the soft grass. She kicked off her shoes and let her feet tangle in the gently swaying blades. She couldn't remember a time when she had felt so relaxed. She closed her eyes and let the warmth and sweetness of her surroundings envelope her.

When her eyes opened again, she was stunned by the dark, mossy forest around her. She was back amongst the oversized trees, and the ground shook. The sound of hundreds or thousands of men marching surrounded her. Through the darkness she could see them, hear their armor clatter and feet crunch the plant life beneath them. They didn't see her, and she followed along. In no time they were at the wall, and the men worked to tear it down. They had built catapults to blast the boulders, and huge ogre-like creatures pulled and pushed, breaking it into pieces. In no time there was a gaping hole in the wall, and the army poured into Charlie's village.

She sat up, confused, before she glanced to where the giant rested with his eyes closed. All at once the memories of the previous day flooded back into her mind. She sighed as she stood, stretched, and packed her things before she disturbed the giant.

Once they were on their way, the giant said, "I had a dream during the night. I saw someone who can help us. But I need you, Little Dreamer, to tell me where to go."

The idea that she, who had never stepped foot outside the wall around her home, would have an idea on where they should go seemed laughable. But Charlie did have an idea.

"I dreamt, too. I saw a meadow; it was so warm and soft. It was perfect…"

The giant grinned. "I know right where that is."

"I had another dream, too, though," Charlie's hands twisted together as she spoke. She told him about her second dream and asked him what it could mean.

"I think the second dream is what would happen if you hadn't come along. I had a very similar dream before I dreamt of you helping me, Charlie."

Charlie sighed, glad that she had chosen to help. She could not let anything bad happen to the people from home, innocent as they were to violence and pain. She had made the right choice to join the giant. At least, she hoped she had.

Chapter 5

Charlie and the giant walked through the forest for several days. The trees became smaller the further away from the river they traveled, until they were the size that Charlie was accustomed to. The giant parted the trees before him like a child parts the tall weeds when tromping through an overgrown field. When she looked behind them, Charlie could see a wake where the giant had broken branches off trees, flattened the undergrowth, and sometimes snapped whole trees in two. Ahead, the forest stretched out in an endless sea of pine and deciduous trees over rolling hills and through river valleys. The view from the giant's shoulder was incredible. It left Charlie speechless as they traveled.

Each day opened new wonders to Charlie. Owls openly hunted for rodents in the night, squirrels could fly from one tree to the next, wild pigs wallowed in mud along a creek bed. There were birds of every different color that sang beautiful songs. Charlie would close her eyes and listen as the music seemed to tell a story, about what, Charlie didn't know. Once a huge golden eagle with a wingspan as long as the giant was tall soared above them. Another time the giant pointed out a herd of centaurs in the distance, that galloped as they shot arrows at whatever it was they were pursuing. In one tree where a chipmunk made a racket, Charlie noticed some tiny human-looking creatures with long, pointed ears attempting to steal nuts from the chipmunk's home.

The forest was noisier than she had expected. There was always the sound of birds and sometimes streams that gurgled, but she also noticed the buzz of a beehive, the slither of an enormous basilisk through the brush of the forest floor, and the chatter of tree rodents as they protested the giant as he disturbed their homes. Charlie loved the coolness of the fresh water from the streams they crossed and was amazed at the size and speed of the river that the giant stepped over, without a break in his stride.

At night they set up makeshift camps, collected bedding for Charlie from the moss and leaves they found, and firewood to give them light and warmth against the darkness.

The giant told Charlie that the reason the giants slept so much was because of a curse. She listened as he told her about a time when his race chose to assist the humans in a great battle, and because of their decision, they had been cursed by an endless sleep.

He said that he hadn't been present for the battle, but that the curse had touched all giants the world over. They had been the predominant peacekeepers of the world, so they had not made their choice lightly. They had saved the world from a great evil, but in so doing, had left various key places and people vulnerable to the remaining wickedness. They had agreed as a race to send guardians to offer as much protection as they could, fighting the cursed sleep and staying awake as long as possible. Thus, the wall around Charlie's home had remained safe for more than five hundred years.

During the day, the pair foraged for food when Charlie's supply from home dwindled. When Charlie's canteen from home ran out, she refilled it with water from the various fresh water sources they came across. She was often nipped by fish or scratched by thorns that grew along the water's edge. She barely noticed that the little scratches, bug bites, and bruises didn't heal as fast as they used to back home; but she did notice that the water didn't taste as pleasant as her own Deep Spring water.

On the fifth night of their journey, the giant confided in Charlie over the campfire. "I'm not excited about the idea of hunting down this army."

Charlie guffawed, then snorted, "Tell me about it!" She laughed some more.

"But I'm glad to be doing something about it," the giant continued. "Instead of waiting for something bad to happen to me."

"I know what you mean. It's scary, but kind of empowering at the same time, right?" Charlie had calmed down. She poked at the fire with a stick, sending sparks into the night.

"Yes. If I had stayed at the wall, they would have come. They would have subdued me and penetrated the wall. I just hope we can figure out who the enemy is and defeat them once and for all."

Charlie agreed. But her heart sank. How could she defeat this mysterious enemy? She was one person, and not a very big one at that. She was no match for an entire army of giant slayers.

As these thoughts troubled her mind, she heard her father's voice in her head, "*You have been chosen for a reason. Make good choices and you will do great things; more than you think you are capable of.*" Charlie hoped he was right. She didn't want to let him down.

The next day they met another of the wild, giant-hunting beasts. It crashed through the trees, and they could see and hear it from quite a distance. The giant slid his sword from his belt, and with one swipe sliced off its head. Charlie's stomach clenched when it happened, but it was over so fast that she didn't have time to react. The giant didn't seem bothered by it at all, and Charlie admired his calmness in the face of danger.

Several days after their encounter with the second ferocious beast, Charlie smelled something sweet as the morning sun warmed the earth around them. Before long they walked into an open meadow with tall grasses, various wildflowers, a rainbow of butterflies, and a deer with her fawn.

"This is the place I saw in my dream!" excitement lifted Charlie's voice.

"Then this is where we will meet the one who can help us," affirmed the giant.

Chapter 6

The giant lowered Charlie to the ground. She took a careful step into the expanse of flowers and breathed in their delicious aroma while she fingered their delicate beauty.

When the giant stepped into the meadow, thousands of butterflies in every shade of reds and blues lifted off the ground and swirled around one another as if in a dance. The butterflies circled over the dewy grass. The light shimmered off each water droplet and reflected the butterflies' rainbow of wings. After they fluttered around the meadow, the butterflies all flew in a gentle motion toward the center. They formed a cloud that was impossible to see through. Then, all at once, they scattered, each flew away in a different direction, and disappeared into the summer sky.

Charlie turned to face the giant. "That was NOT in my dream."

The giant opened his mouth as if to reply but closed it again. His eyes had fixed onto something behind Charlie. She turned to see what he gaped at.

A human sized fairy descended from the middle of the cloud of butterflies. She had always thought fairies were small beings, but her research on the subject had been in a book about mythical creatures, so it was possible her assumptions were wrong.

The sun was to the woman's back which casted her front in shadow. Her wavy, golden hair floated around her as she lowered to the ground with her great, iridescent wings. She alighted on one pointed toe and stepped forward with her other bare foot. She landed with the poise of a dancer before Charlie.

Charlie stepped back as several huge, fuzzy legs unwrapped themselves from the fairy's torso. A giant white butterfly flapped in slow motion as it whisked

away. The white stripes on the woman's silky, lavender dress were gone. She wasn't a fairy at all, but a human woman. Charlie choked back an astonished laugh.

As the woman made her way towards Charlie and the giant, animals of all different kinds flocked to her. In a matter of minutes several butterflies landed on her woven-lavender crown, a red winged black bird sang and hovered above her, a fawn poked at her skirts. A few dozen bees buzzed above her head and a couple of fuzzy black and gold caterpillars crawled up her dress. A skunk rubbed against her ankles for attention.

The woman looked at the giant as she neared, a joyous look spread across her face. She stretched her arms out and her pace quickened. She seemed to dance towards them. When she got closer, she rushed toward the giant and wrapped her delicate arms around one of his wide legs in a warm, welcome hug. The animals had followed her and still circled her or rubbed their noses against her. She released the giant and stepped back several paces to peer at him.

She cupped her hands around her crimson lips and called in a sweet voice, "Dear giant, I am so glad to see you!" As she spoke, she brushed the bird off her shoulder and nudged the skunk away with one foot.

Charlie looked at the giant. He looked bewildered. Charlie walked to the woman and blushed, "Um, hi…"

The woman twirled around, clasped her hands together in front of her chest and let out a sigh. "I cannot believe a giant has come to visit me! I am so honored. What a delightful day this has turned out to be. Did you two like the butterfly show?"

"Yeah… Um, do you know him?" Charlie asked as she gestured toward the giant.

"Well, no… but does it matter? He is a giant! Here!" she squealed.

The woman took a step closer to Charlie while she waved the butterflies away from her face with one hand. She whispered something to the bees and picked up the caterpillars with her other hand before she set them on a nearby daylily. She extended her left hand in introduction and greeted Charlie with her bright blue eyes. "I am Princess Juliette. I am pleased to make your acquaintance. And you are…?"

"Oh. Um. I'm Charlie." Charlie was taken aback by Princess Juliette. She half expected her to start singing to the animals at any moment. She appeared to be too perfect to be real. And the way she had floated in on a giant butterfly combined with the animals flocking around her was even more peculiar.

"It is indeed a pleasure to meet you today, Charlie. I so much look forward to learning more about you!" Juliette's voice was overly cheerful. Juliette looked at the giant again and continued, "And I look forward to spending time with your travel companion. You must tell me all about yourselves!" The woman never stopped smiling.

The giant squatted to better hear the conversation, and seemed to be as perplexed by Juliette as Charlie was.

"So, you are the Princess. I have heard of you before. You are the caretaker of all living creatures," the giant said.

"That is right!" answered Juliette, still smiling at them.

Charlie would have expected someone who was a caretaker of animals to be dressed more practical. And to enjoy the attention she received from the animals still around her. As it was, she seemed bothered by them. Charlie didn't understand this contrast but hoped that this happy person could help them. Somehow.

"You both simply must stay the night here with me. I will have the meadow people prepare a delicious feast, and we shall all bask in the glow of a warm fire while we talk into the night of your journey. And we will become dear, dear friends." Juliette had a faraway look in her eyes. She refocused on her two visitors. "You will stay, will you not?" she asked in a worried but hopeful voice.

"Yes. We would be happy to accept your invitation," the giant answered as Charlie nodded. Her curiosity won out. She looked forward to finding out more about Juliette.

Juliette led her guests across the meadow to the edge of the forest on the other side. All the while the animals closed in on the Princess, and she pushed them away like she wanted to pretend they weren't there. She let out a gentle whistle and another person emerged from the trees.

"Ivy," Juliette spoke to the new person, "how are the rabbit burrows turning out? Do you think they will be finished before the babies arrive?" She bounced with excitement as she spoke.

"Oh yes, Your Highness. They are coming along fine." Ivy answered, clear pleasure shone through her words. She wore green linen trousers and shirt, along with soft moccasins and a woven shade hat. Her appearance was much more practical, what Charlie would've expected someone who cares for animals to look like. "Would you like to come see?" Ivy took a step back in the direction she had come and invited them to follow.

"I would, but just not at the moment," the Princess answered. "Thank you for the invitation. Speaking of rabbit burrows, I would like you to meet my new, dear friends." She gestured behind her at Charlie and behind Charlie, the giant. Juliette beamed from ear to ear as she introduced her guests.

Chapter 7

After a short nap, Charlie stood and stretched as she walked to the edge of an amphitheater. It had been an empty, grassy hill over a flat dirt area when she had fallen asleep. Now there were strings of daisies winding up and down the hillside, and fireflies perched on the poles prepared to add light to the upcoming entertainment. Low tables had been arranged around the entire semi-circle at the base of the hill. Three banquet-sized tables made of long, flat boulders anchored the center. The entire base of the hill was decorated, and torches were arranged for additional lighting. People were busy making preparations, all of them dressed much the same as Ivy had been.

Juliette returned after a couple of hours and invited her guests to join her at the center table below for a feast. As she spoke, the workers all gathered around the tables, with more people joining them from the forest.

The giant chose to stay where he was, and Charlie hoped he wouldn't feel left out. He didn't seem to care all that much, but she decided to remember what they talked about so she could tell him everything word for word when she joined him again later. She followed

Juliette down the slope and toward the center table. Juliette gestured for Charlie to take the seat next to her, and Charlie waited to sit until Juliette did. Wasn't that the proper protocol when visiting with royalty?

Everyone else stood beside the table and watched as Juliette clapped her hands to call attention to herself. She introduced Charlie and the giant to everyone present and invited everyone to have a seat. Charlie sat on the soft ground beside Juliette and crossed her legs underneath her. A young man with wild blonde hair that had green streaks throughout brought Juliette and Charlie each a thick leaf the size of a dinner plate loaded with all kinds of delicious fruit salads, steamed and roasted root vegetables, tossed leafy greens, and a variety of nuts and legumes. He bowed to Juliette before he took two backwards steps and rejoined his friends at a different table.

Charlie waited for Juliette to eat before she took a bite of some of the food before her. She watched all the others around her as they joked around with one another, talked with smiling heads close together, and enjoyed their time. She remembered what it felt like to be a part of a group, but it had been a very long time. She observed as everyone had so much fun with their friends.

Because everyone else where Charlie was from didn't retain memories, it had been hard for her to establish lasting friendships. When she was a child, she played with whoever was nearby. If they shared an interest, they were best friends. But as she grew, it became more awkward. Her friends couldn't remember what they had done together in the past, or secrets they had shared. Charlie could. She would often reference something that her friends couldn't remember, and they would give her strange looks. As they grew, her peers started to think she was weird, or had a too-vivid imagination. Or that she was a liar. She grew apart from the others and soon her only friend was her father. She wished he were here now, to see this amazing place and meet all these interesting people.

One of the young men that sat across the table from Charlie caught her eye. He talked with his friend, then turned toward Charlie. His dark brown eyes matched his hair and skin, and Charlie could tell he was tall, even while he sat. His clothes were a light, breathable linen that was the color of the meadow grass, and his sleeves were short and exposed his strong arms and hands.

"Hello, Charlie, I'm Alder. It's nice to meet you." His eyes crinkled and he grinned as he reached across the table to shake her hand.

"It's nice to meet you, too." Charlie stumbled over the words as she returned the handshake. She wasn't used to meeting new people, and this was the first person she had met that was close to her own age. Though she had lived five hundred years, in most ways she was still a teenager. She blushed as she tried to think of something to say.

"It's good to have visitors. How long are you planning to stay?" Alder continued the conversation in an easy way.

"I'm not sure, maybe a few days…" Charlie trailed off.

"I wish I could stay longer," Alder replied. "Unfortunately, I must leave early tomorrow morning."

"Oh, you don't live here?" Charlie asked.

"This is the home of the fauna caretakers. I work with plants. I am just stopping by for a visit. I was quite pleased to have come on a banquet night. Lucky me!" he winked at Charlie.

Charlie blushed, again, and didn't know what to say. Why did she have to be so bad at small talk?

Someone came up behind Alder and spoke softly to him. He turned to Charlie with a sad look, "I'm afraid I must excuse myself. I do wish we had more time to talk." He did look regretful.

"I understand." Charlie watched Alder stand and walk away. He glanced back at her and waved over his shoulder.

Charlie caught herself staring and shook herself out of her trance. She turned to Juliette instead and asked, "So, you take care of animals here?"

Juliette sat straighter and her voice became bubbly. "Oh, yes! We do so much! We offer protection for the weaker animals and ensure that the animal kingdom functions as it should. We are ultimately responsible for all the animals and plant life of our world. I especially love the baby animals. They are so cute and cuddly!"

"Are there more of you? Do you take care of all animals, or just the animals right here?" Charlie wanted to know.

"There are other groups of my people scattered across the world."

The enthusiasm Juliette displayed for her role seemed contrary to what Charlie had observed about Juliette. Her clothing was elegant, not functional. She seemed distracted and bothered by the attention she received from the animals. But when she talked about the work her people do, she lit up.

"Is this where you live?" Charlie asked next.

"Oh yes, my group lives here, on the edge of this meadow. I have several relatives who are in charge of other groups. Some help near the sea, others work high on cliffs, some work with hibernating animals, we work here with forest creatures. What about you, Charlie, where are you from?"

Charlie swallowed the food in her mouth. How much should she share about where she was from or about her purpose for her being here with the giant? But the giant had said that Juliette would be able to help them. That meant she needed to trust her, too. At least a little.

"I come from quite far away, where the plants are much bigger. My friend and I are traveling to find out what has happened to the other giants. He is being tracked by some strange beasts, and we are trying to figure out where they are coming from."

Juliette startled; her smile gone. "Can you describe these creatures for me?" Juliette's voice was low and full of concern.

Charlie described the creatures for Juliette, alarmed at her reaction. "Do you know what they are?" Her heart beat faster.

"I do not know what they are or where they came from, but I have had reports of a new kind of creature roaming around as of late." Juliette's eyes darkened. Her hands trembled. "It has disturbed me. I am aware of all living things but do not know anything about these. I have some ideas, but have not seen one for myself, and so have not been able to learn more."

She paused and looked thoughtful. "I believe if I could have physical contact with one, I would be able to form a connection with its mind and discover something about its origin. They have disrupted the balance of nature, and I must find out what they are doing here if things are to return to normal."

"I don't think you'll have much luck being able to touch one of them. They are pretty vicious," Charlie commented.

"Yes, that does present a problem. Perhaps your companion would have some suggestions about this." She stood and motioned for Charlie to do the same. "I believe it is time we move away from the festivities and consult him together to formulate a plan."

Charlie listened quietly as Juliette and the giant talked about the creatures and the giant's encounters with them. They discussed different ways they would be able to capture one.

"I need the creature to be alive in order for me to connect with it, but it must be calm, as well," Juliette explained.

"Does it need to be awake?" the giant wanted to know.

"No, that would not be necessary."

"What if you knocked one out," suggested the giant.

"That should work," Juliette said. "Would you be able to do that?"

"Me?" the giant sounded surprised. "I thought you might have some way to do it."

Juliette shook her head. "I may be able to come up with something given enough time and planning, but it would be much faster to have you take care of it. Do not worry, my great friend, I have faith in you! If you can do me this great favor, I will be able to discover these creatures' story, and I may be able to alter their vicious inclinations."

Juliette turned to Charlie. "I would hope that you could assist the giant. After the creature is unconscious, could you help tie a net and ropes around it? I do not believe the giant could do this with his large hands. Once you have it bound, the giant can carry it back to me."

The giant looked at Charlie. He looked nervous while he waited for her to answer. She hesitated. "Yes, I will help. But I'm wondering, wouldn't some of your people be more suited for the job?"

"Ideally, yes. They would. However, as part of our stewardship we must not willingly harm another living creature. We would lose our ability to communicate and aid all creatures by doing so. It is simply not worth the sacrifice."

Charlie let this sink in. "I guess we don't really have a choice. We'll have to do what we can."

The giants face fell. "I agree to the plan as well."

Juliette clapped her hands together and another huge smile lit up her face. "Oh! Thank you!" She invited them to join the rest of her people for the entertainment.

They sat in the center of the amphitheater hillside to watch the show. Juliette had arranged for several groups of her people to put on a performance with the animals they cared for. A group of birds sang for the crowd. A peacock strutted across the stage, opening and closing its fan of beautiful tail feathers, shaking them as it twirled. A falcon flew low over the heads of the audience before it climbed high into the air, swooped with incredible speed, and pulled up as Charlie thought for sure it was going to crash into the ground. The crowd cheered and encouraged the animals as they performed and received praise from those who were their caretakers.

Charlie watched as a man stepped onto the stage and the crowd fell silent. He was dressed in dark clothing, and carried a large, red bird in his arms. The bird looked scraggly, and a feather fell out of it as the man set it carefully in a nest that had been placed in the center of the stage. What could this sick-looking bird possibly do that would be entertaining? The crowd around Charlie leaned forward, silent. Charlie jumped in her seat when the bird burst into flames, and the theater filled with "oohs" and "aahs."

Charlie's throat tightened. The bird had burned to a pile of ashes. She felt sick as the eyes of the people seemed glued to the stage. This was all at odds with the fact that they were the caretakers of the animal kingdom. Had she been tricked somehow? Were these people good, or were they bad? Just as she was about to leave her seat, she heard a chirping noise come from the ashes. She leaned forward to look more carefully at the singed nest. There, in the ashes, was a tiny, featherless baby bird with large red eyes.

"A phoenix!" Charlie whispered to herself.

"Oh, yes, Charlie!" Juliette answered. Charlie had forgotten that the Princess was beside her. Juliette continued, "They are rare, and it is a privilege to be able to observe its rebirth." Juliette's voice was barely above a whisper. Her face was filled with reverence, and she didn't take her own eyes off the amazing bird.

The man in the dark clothing picked up the entire nest, bowed to the audience, and returned into the shadows.

The crowd erupted in a standing ovation, and Charlie was once again in awe of the world in which she found herself.

Chapter 8

When the show was over and the applause had died down, Juliette showed Charlie where she could sleep for the night. Some of Juliette's people had arranged a room for Charlie beneath the roots of a large rowan tree. Soft pillows stuffed with the down shed from baby geese and wrapped in silk spun by thousands of silkworms formed the bed. She had a blanket woven from the wool of angora llamas, which was soft to the touch and warm when wrapped around her.

This place felt like a palace! She had been sleeping on the ground in the forest for over a week now. She settled into this cozy bed, and it didn't take long for her to fall asleep.

Charlie walked through a crowded, dark city. The buildings were taller than any she had seen before. The people she encountered were disfigured and cruel. They snarled at her and called her names. They crowded around her, reached their hands out to grab her. She turned and ran away from them. Her feet pounded on the cobblestone street and the sound echoed off the walls. She kept checking over her shoulder. Every time there were more people and strange creatures. The walls closed in around her. How was she going to escape?

On one side of the cobblestone street, she saw a sign ahead, illuminated by the sun, for a pawnbroker's shop. She ran through the door to the shop and slammed it behind her. Her heart raced as she tried to catch her breath.

Before Charlie was a room filled with trinkets and furniture of all shapes and sizes.

A moment later a woman with very curly black hair and a smile that did not reach her eyes came out from behind a curtain at the back of the shop. Something about the look on her face caused Charlie to recoil.

The woman opened her mouth and was about to say something to Charlie.

Just as the words started, Charlie woke.

With a sigh, she turned to one side to look through the tree roots to where the sky turned from pink to blue as the sun rose. She leaned on one elbow and thought about her dream. She still needed to calm down. It had been claustrophobic in the city she had wandered through, the crowd of people that had chased her, and the shop she had found herself in. She tried to shake off her anxiety. She stood to breathe in the fresh morning air.

Charlie remembered what she had agreed to do with the giant and groaned. She didn't want to go out into the forest in the hopes of coming across another one of those terrifying creatures. She didn't know how long it would take and felt like it was a waste of time. Even if they were able to attract one, would they be able to knock it out, tie it up, and bring it back? And if they did, would Juliette be able to find out what they needed to know?

And she was anxious about the woman in the dream. Was she someone who could help them? And what did that little prick of fear mean that the woman's eyes had stoked in Charlie?

The weight of everything pressed on Charlie. She stepped out of the tree roots into the morning light to find her traveling companion.

Chapter 9

Charlie was greeted by Juliette and provided with a delicious breakfast of fruit and milk from a large nut-like pod. Juliette made sure Charlie had all the supplies she needed for their plan to capture the beast. She had packed a large bag with ropes and nets and included food and water and a soft blanket for overnight. The giant slid the bag onto his belt and Charlie once again rode on his shoulder for their trek.

On the second day, Charlie and the giant could hear one of the beasts from a distance. Horrified by the thought of another encounter with one of these creatures, Charlie's stomach did a flip. She recalled her narrow escape from the first time.

Charlie signaled for the giant to remove the bag of supplies from his belt. Charlie hurried to unload its contents and prepared to wrap the creature. She stood behind the giant, ready to dart forward and bind the creature's legs and mouth.

The beast crashed through the brush into the clearing. The giant slammed his hands onto the creature, like a child traps a grasshopper. His fear for her obviously clouded his judgment. He hit the creature harder than Charlie thought necessary. She stepped from around the giant and looked at his face as he crouched to the ground.

His face looked surprised. Charlie watched as he peeked under his hands. She braced herself with the ropes, ready to spring forward. But the giant lifted his hands and shot a guilty look at Charlie. She took a tentative look at where the creature lay and whirled around to face the giant.

"You squished it!" Charlie cried.

"Sorry," the giant kept his head low, focused on the ground. "It was an accident."

Charlie let out a sigh. Now they'd have to wait for another one. She wanted to get this over with.

"I didn't mean to."

"I know." Charlie tried really hard to not sound as annoyed as she felt. "We'll just have to hope that another one will come along soon."

She did not want to look at the creature, or what was left of it, any longer, so she turned around and walked into the forest.

"Want to ride?"

"Sure." She allowed the giant to help her onto his shoulder once more. They walked the rest of the day and camped for another night.

Charlie slept near the fire. It had died down to a pile of embers, and the air had a hint of smoke in it. Charlie snuggled into her blanket while she dreamed about fighting off dozens of the beasts. In her restless sleep she had a vague awareness of a noise in the forest, but it was part of her dream.

The noise grew closer and the ground shook. She awoke and threw her blanket from her. Adrenaline coursed through her and chased away all thoughts of sleep. She heard the creature snarl and snap its jaws as it ran full force toward the clearing.

She fumbled around for her dagger. This was no dream. She raised it in defense. The creature's saliva sprayed her face. It was just out of her reach. It was going to crash into her.

She crouched and hid under her arms. She screamed for the giant. The creature swiped at her with razor sharp claws. Pain ripped through Charlie's forearm. She collapsed.

In an instant the attack ended, and the creature was silent.

Charlie lifted her head from the ground. Tears blurred her vision. She rubbed her eyes with her left arm and cradled her right arm against her body. She looked into the giant's face, just being able to make out his features from the soft glow from the remains of the fire.

"Charlie…" the giant whispered.

Charlie curled in on herself, hugging her legs close to her body, and favored her wounded arm. Her body shook with sobs.

"I am so sorry," the giant still spoke in a whisper.

Charlie did not respond. She kept her head low and wouldn't make eye contact with the giant. She did, however, glance at the creature, which, to her surprise, was not dead, but lay in a crumpled, unconscious heap on the ground.

After a long time, her breath slowed and she squeaked, "It's not dead?"

"No, I knocked it out."

Charlie's throat was tight, but she managed to not lose herself to crying again. "I guess we should secure it?"

The giant nodded. "But I'll need your help." He looked so guilty.

Charlie didn't want to go near the creature. She also didn't want to help the giant. Not really.

Where had he been? Why hadn't he stopped the creature before it attacked her? She could have died!

"Charlie?" the giant asked.

"What?" she replied flatly.

"We should act fast, before it wakes up." His voice was sheepish.

Charlie stood. She winced from the pain in her arm.

The giant handed her the bag with the ropes and nets. The pair worked in silence. The giant draped the net on top of the creature and rolled it over to envelope the beast. Next, Charlie worked the rope through the net and around the creature. She moved with caution as she maneuvered around it. She held her injured arm close to her body. Her blood seeped into her shirt.

When they finished securing the creature, Charlie spread the sack on the ground so the giant could put the brute into it. He pulled the sides and Charlie tied the sack closed. The giant set it behind a nearby tree, out of sight, and turned back toward Charlie.

The sun was just beginning to lighten the sky as he knelt beside Charlie. He begged her with his eyes to speak to him.

Tears slid down her face. "Where were you?" She cradled her arm again.

"I am truly sorry, Charlie."

"Seriously? That's all you have to say?"

"I should not have left you alone."

"You think?"

"I understand why you are angry with me. It was foolish of me to leave you."

"But why? Why did you leave?"

"I needed to think. Then I slept. I woke when you screamed. I wasn't that far away. But my mind was not here, and that was dangerous. I promise not to fail you again."

Charlie didn't respond. She turned her back to him and pulled out some supplies. She needed to clean and dress her wound as best as she could. It hurt more than she had ever experienced, and it didn't heal liked back home. Every movement shot pain up and down her arm. Breathless from it she reached for the packet from her father and removed the vial of Deep Spring water. She held it in her hand. Should she drink it? Is this why her father had given it to her? Surely, he would have seen this attack and not wanted her to have to suffer without the healing effects of the water.

She pulled the cork stopper out of the vial and lifted it to her mouth.

"STOP!" the giant shouted. It scared Charlie half to death. "Don't drink it, please!"

"First you leave me here to get attacked by that thing, and then you stop me from making the pain go away?" Her normally dormant temper started to flare.

"Please, I know it's tempting. But now is not the time. Save the water." The giant's voice was calm, which only infuriated Charlie more.

"Why?" Charlie demanded. "Is there something you know that you're not telling me?"

The giant didn't answer right away. "I just know you shouldn't drink it now. Your arm will heal. The pain will recede. Please, just give it time."

Now she wanted to drink the water just to spite him! But something about the way he told her to stop made her think that she might regret it later. She glared at him as she put the cork back and tucked it away in her pack once more. She used her other supplies to clean her arm.

She grimaced as she washed out the deep gashes with regular water. Her blood turned it pink as it ran off her arm. She bit her tongue to stifle a cry when she wrapped it tight with dry cloth and knotted it with her uninjured hand and teeth.

When she finished, she gathered all of her things and stuffed them back into her pack. "Let's go."

The giant sighed, but picked up the sack with the creature and flung it onto his back. He followed Charlie back through the forest the way they had come. They walked all day and through part of the night. They made it back to Juliette's meadow before the moon was high in the sky.

Charlie watched in silence as the giant set the sack down before Juliette and some of her people. Charlie turned toward her temporary home under the tree. She asked for a change of clothes and cleaned herself up. Then she curled up in bed. Her arm throbbed and her heart hurt. She fell asleep as her mind stewed.

Chapter 10

Charlie was back in the city with the tall buildings and disturbing inhabitants. She stood in a courtyard and people ran all around like crazy. It was chaos. People screamed and waved their arms, bumped into one another, and knocked each other over. Charlie's hands covered her ears as she attempted to block out the sound of some kind of alarm. Just as she thought things couldn't get any crazier, the city began to fall apart. It was as if the ground beneath the city had collapsed.

People disappeared in sinkholes, whole buildings crumbled and fell, shouts rang out all around as people scattered in all directions. It was a strange sensation to be surrounded by so many people but feel so out of place.

Charlie only witnessed the destruction. She wasn't harmed by it, and people ran right past her. The view changed so that she looked over the edge of a cliff at the sea. Others peered over the cliff with her. Water splashed impossibly high from below. Just as it was about to plummet to the ground and soak Charlie, she woke from her dream.

Charlie patted herself. She should be wet but found herself dry and still safely tucked away in her temporary bedroom.

She managed to go back to sleep not long after. Maybe she would gain more insight from her dreams. But she slept without another dream for the rest of the night.

When she woke in the morning, she did not feel refreshed. Glimpses from her dream flashed in her memory, but the images were so scattered. She couldn't get her mind to grasp onto a single event long enough to place it in a sequence, let alone figure out what it might mean.

She couldn't help but be troubled by what had happened with the beast they had captured, and her subsequent anger with the giant. The combination of both of these intense emotional events and the pain from her injury left her drained.

Charlie stayed in bed and pondered over everything in her sleepy mind. Soon, a messenger of Juliette's approached and invited her to come speak with Juliette.

Charlie was led to Juliette's quarters and the messenger tapped on the door. Charlie was shocked at Juliette's appearance. She didn't look as perky as she had before. Her skin was pale and eyes puffy. She wore her same silky lavender dress, but there were no flowery adornments this morning. Instead of curls cascading over her shoulders and down her back, her hair was pulled back in a low ponytail and a few curly tendrils framed her face.

"Charlie, thank you so much for coming. Please, do come in and have a seat." Her voice sounded weary.

Charlie followed Juliette into the space. Plush cushions and soft blankets dotted the room; a thick bed of wool covered with lavender and ringed with sandalwood nestled in the corner. The morning light shone through openings high up in the walls and filled the room with a warm glow.

Juliette led Charlie to a cluster of pillows around a low wooden table. A teapot made from a dried gourd rested on the table. Alongside the teapot of aromatic tea sat a tray of scones loaded with dried fruit

"Would you like some rosemary tea?" Juliette asked as she picked up the pot and poured hot water into the cup nearest her.

Charlie accepted the offer and Juliette poured water into a second cup and handed it to her. Charlie lifted the cup to her mouth and blew on the steaming tea. She inhaled the delicious aroma with eyes closed before she took a sip.

"Speaking of rosemary tea," Juliette began. "I must apologize for meeting with you in my quarters. I do prefer to hold meetings in much more open, beautiful spaces. But the information I have gathered from the beast was quite distressing to me, and I very much prefer that our conversation not be overheard. I do not wish to incite fear into my people, and I cannot be certain that there are not spies present at any given time," Juliette paused to take another sip of tea.

"Spies? Here? Isn't everyone here loyal to you?" Charlie's teacup was frozen halfway to her mouth. Her eyes were wide.

"Oh, the people here are loyal, as are most of the animals. But I can never be certain what animals may lurk in the forest, listening and watching. And after what I have seen, I do not dare to take a risk that anything we discuss be revealed to those who wish us harm.

"Would you care for an elderberry and blueberry scone?" Juliette extended the platter toward Charlie.

"Oh, sure," Charlie replied. She carefully placed a scone on the plate next to her teacup and broke off a piece to eat.

"Shall I continue?" Juliette asked.

Charlie nodded.

"Very well," Juliette set her cup on the table. She tucked her feet under her to one side as she shifted into a more comfortable position.

Charlie watched and listened as Juliette used both hands and her expressive face to fill in Charlie. She explained to Charlie that she simply needed to touch an animal's head, and she could connect with it on a subconscious level, seeing it's memories as if they were her own. It usually left her physically exhausted, but it helped her understand problems that animals may be having and allowed her to help them.

Her experience with the dark creature had been unpleasant, and Juliette had not been able to maintain her connection for very long.

Juliette sighed as she finished. Her eyes were focused on some imaginary place in the distance, and Charlie knew that Juliette was reliving her experience. She didn't envy Juliette's gift. She didn't think she would be able to handle the lives and feelings of endless numbers of creatures.

"Anyway," Juliette refocused her eyes on Charlie. Her expression was still serious, and Charlie worried about what she would hear. "Let me tell you what I saw, and what I believe it means.

"This creature does not have a very long memory. It is very young, but its body functions as a mature animal. From the creature's eyes I saw a pack of other animals just like this one. They were snarling and snapping and fighting over food. Someone appeared and spoke a word of command, and as one the pack ran through dark tunnels and out into the open."

Charlie noticed that Juliette grew more agitated the longer she talked. Her hands were clasped tight in her lap, and her breathing grew steadily faster as she spoke.

"The animals ran together; the leader smelled the air and barked directions to the pack. Soon the pack split into pairs, and the one we have here stayed with the leader. It was being trained.

"The pair ran for a terribly long time, but never seemed to tire. Soon enough they had found the quarry they were tracking. They attacked their prey, keeping him occupied for some time.

"Presently an army of men came into view. At that, the creatures backed away as the men attacked and destroyed what they had hunted. The creatures were leading this army of men."

Juliette looked away briefly and swallowed hard before she continued her story. "At first, I was not exactly sure how, but after sifting through several other memories of this creature tracking and locating its prey, I found the memory that is the key to all. A face appeared before me, before the creature. It is the creature's creator and master. This revelation startled me so much that my connection to the creature was abruptly disconnected."

Charlie waited. Juliette didn't say any more.

"Why? What did you see?" Charlie asked.

Juliette's voice broke with a sob. "There is a vast army of humans that are using these creatures to hunt, and to slay, the giants."

Chapter 11

This information confirmed what the giant had suspected all along. Charlie knew little about this world that she had fallen in to, and it was still hard to wrap her mind around the fact that there were people who would want to harm and destroy giants. Her friend was so calm and humble. He didn't have a mean bone in his enormous body.

"Why would they want to kill the giants?" Charlie blurted out.

"I have learned from the shared knowledge of these dark beasts that they have just recently begun hunting the giants. The giants are the peacekeepers in our world, but I am not certain of the reason why they are leading the men to kill them, for the majority of the giants are under an enchanted sleep."

Charlie nodded. This she already knew.

Juliette continued, "They have not succeeded in tracking most of the giants yet, and if you and your giant friend can awaken all of the remaining giants, this enemy may be defeated."

Charlie nodded. Then stopped. "Wait, what?" What could Juliette mean by this? Awaken the giants? "How are we supposed to wake up sleeping giants, exactly? I thought we would, I don't know, find the bad guy or something."

"I have pondered this as well." Juliette's feet returned to the floor, and she sat up a little taller. "There is a way. The risk is great, and the chances of success are small, but knowing what I know, it would be unwise to sit idly by and allow evil to conquer. The results would be devastating to all living things, human and animal alike. If the person who has created these beasts succeeds in killing most or all of the sleeping giants, then they would be one step closer to obtaining great power. And one who obtains power through manipulation and murder is not one who should have power to begin with. I have no doubt that this person intends to continue their path of destruction in hopes to rule many, if not all, of the people and creatures of this world. This must not happen.

"I know what must be done, but I am afraid to ask you to do it." Juliette could hold the tears back no longer, and Charlie watched as the Princess closed her eyes and the tears slid in a steady, silent stream down her face.

Charlie didn't like the sound of any of this. Juliette was afraid to ask Charlie to proceed? Then how dangerous was it? And why couldn't Juliette, or one of her own people, do it?

Before she had a chance to voice her concerns, however, Juliette spoke once more. "Without your help," the Princess choked out, "evil will prevail, and all living things will suffer a great deal. The world will be changed forever. We have an advantage that I am sure these giant-slayers are unaware of, and there is a chance for good to overcome.

"You have a gift, Charlie. You are a Dreamer. Which gives you tremendous advantage over this enemy."

Charlie sat quiet and let everything Juliette had told her sink in. Maybe her dreams, her journey through the wall, encountering the giant and agreeing to help him, had all led her to Juliette. The one who had the ability to read the minds of animals, including the giant-hunting beasts. If she hadn't done that, they would not have discovered this dark plan nor would they be able to figure out a way to stop the giant-slayers.

Charlie resigned herself to the fact that this was what she was meant to do. "Princess, what can I do?"

Juliette took a deep breath. The flow of tears down her rosy cheeks slowed. Her pale hands shook as she wiped the remaining wetness away and looked at Charlie. "I know what needs to be done. It is a difficult task for anyone, but I believe that you are the one that is meant to do it. I believe that is why you have come."

"I know," Charlie testified. She met Juliette's eye. Her voice was calm but sure.

"The face that I saw is the center of everything. All that she does is selfish. I believe if you can locate her, you will find what you will need in order to awaken the slumbering giants."

"She?" The face behind this darkness was a woman?

"Charlie, evil has many faces. That is how it hides so easily."

Charlie couldn't keep all of this straight. She didn't understand what she was supposed to do. She asked Juliette to explain.

"There is an item you need to find. Legend calls it the Battle Horn, and it belongs to the giants. In addition to creating these unnatural creatures and hunting and slaying the giants, I can only assume she is searching for the Battle Horn in order to prevent any giant from using it, for to use this device would result in the amassing of an army of giants which would fight back. This would be devastating to the giant-slayers.

"In addition to preventing use of this device by the giants, any person who held it in their possession would have immediate power over the leaders of the cities. This device is legendary, but she is counting on the fact that it exists."

"So, does it? Exist?"

"Oh, yes, Charlie. I know for a fact that it does. In the wrong hands it would be a terrible tool, but in the right hands," Juliette leaned forward and looked deep into Charlie's eyes, "it would be an invaluable asset, more or less guaranteeing a victory over this evil force. But it must be found and used with haste, before there are not enough giants left to fight back."

"So.... This is where I come in?" Charlie swallowed hard. How was she going to be the one to do all of this?

"Yes. You will need to seek her out. I do not know where she can be found, but I believe you can discover her location through your dreams. The woman's name is Jessamine. And, Charlie? She is not to be trusted."

The images of Charlie's most recent dreams about the city, and the woman with the untrustworthy eyes, flashed into Charlie's mind. But she still had one question to ask.

"Princess?" she wondered out loud, "How do you know who she is, you said you only saw her face for a moment?"

"Because," Juliette responded, jaw set and eyes filled with sorrow. "She is my cousin."

Chapter 12

Juliette told Charlie the story of how she knew Jessamine, and how their relationship had gone from closer-than-sisters to never seeing one another again.

The girls had grown up together. Jessamine had been Juliette's best friend and confidant. Juliette loved her cousin, and the two had grown ever closer during their young years. Juliette told Charlie that the summer the girls were both thirteen years old, Jessamine had made a choice that had led her down a path of darkness.

The young teenage girls, not much younger than Charlie effectively was now, had been sitting near a stream, their dresses splayed out around them, their hair disheveled from the race they had just finished before collapsing in a fit of giggles. They were carefree, not thinking about their future responsibilities, or anything that might weigh down their good moods.

They ate their apples and giggled over the cute new gardener that had given them the apples that morning. They stretched out on the ground, arms underneath their heads, pointing out shapes in the clouds floating across the blue summer sky.

Juliette became thirsty and made her way to the creek. She kneeled and cupped her hands to drink. Jessamine joined her, and the two began communicating with the animals in and around the creek. Juliette talked to a dragonfly, while Jessamine interacted with a young rainbow trout.

The dragonfly flew away and Juliette turned to see the fish doing flips in the air.

"Jess! What are you doing?!" cried Juliette.

Jessamine allowed the fish to fall back into the water and swim frantically away. "What? It's no big deal," she shrugged her shoulders with a smirk.

"Yes, it is!" Juliette frowned. "You were making the fish do that."

"So what?" Jessamine wanted to know.

"Why were you doing that?" Juliette responded with her own question.

"Because it was funny." Jessamine squirmed under her cousin's disapproval.

"It was not funny, not at all!"

"Geesh, Jules, lighten up. I was just playing around. I didn't hurt it or anything!" Jessamine scowled; her countenance darker.

"Jess, communicating with the animals is a gift. We are supposed to use it to help them, not control them. We are charged to be selfless with our power. You were being selfish."

Jessamine stood and plunked her hands on her hips. "I don't see what the big deal is. You are freaking out about nothing."

"It is not nothing, Jessamine. Do not do it again." Juliette stood to face her cousin.

"Well, *Juliette*, I'll do my best to not disappoint you again," Jessamine sneered. She tossed her long, dark hair and glared at her cousin.

"Jess, my position gives me stewardship over the animals. You have to understand." Juliette's voice softened as she tried to let Jessamine know she wasn't mad.

"Whatever, *Your Highness*," Jessamine mocked, and she turned her back on Juliette and stalked away.

"Jess, wait!" Juliette had called. But Jessamine ignored her.

Nothing had been the same between them after that. Jessamine wouldn't speak to Juliette unless she had to, no matter how hard Juliette had tried. Their relationship was strained, until a few years later, when Jessamine left one night without saying good-bye.

Jessamine's life had been consumed with seeking power over others. Juliette wished she could have helped her cousin choose a different way. Juliette had believed Jessamine to be no longer living, as she hadn't heard anything about her in many years. She was startled to discover she was wrong.

Charlie's heart hurt for her new friend. How must she feel, if her cousin, whom Charlie could tell she cared about very much, was the one behind all of this? She wanted to reassure Juliette that she was ready to help.

She sat up. "Princess, I saw a city in my dream. I think I know where to go!"

Juliette looked stunned. "You saw it?"

"Yes, and I also saw a woman. She had dark hair and dark eyes. She was young but seemed mature in her mannerisms."

"That is Jessamine. Do not let her youthful appearance deceive you. She is a dangerous woman. Would you mind telling me about your dreams?"

Charlie agreed and gave Juliette the details she could remember. As she spoke, the color returned to Juliette's face and she stood.

"Hope is not lost, then." They worked out a strategy and assigned tasks to Juliette's subjects to gather supplies and ready Charlie and the giant for their journey.

Charlie sought out the giant as soon as she left Juliette's quarters. All tension between the two friends dissolved, Charlie having forgotten about her anger. Her arm was slowly on the mend, though still tender and raw underneath the bandage. Juliette had given her a poultice to smear on it for the pain and for quicker healing, for which Charlie was grateful. But their new task pushed all other thoughts and worries from her mind. She invited her friend to take a walk with her so she could tell him everything.

After they entered the grove of rowan trees, the giant lifted Charlie onto his shoulder. Charlie told him about her conversation with Juliette. At first the giant was speechless. In fact, upon learning the details about how many giants the army had already slain, he stopped. But with some urging from Charlie, he continued his stroll. Charlie shared with him everything that Juliette had told her, as well as about her recent dreams. When she finished, the giant was quiet.

"What are you thinking?" Charlie asked, nervous about his reaction.

"I don't know…"

Charlie noticed a new clench to his jaw and tension in his neck and shoulders. She knew there would be no stopping him on this quest to save his fellow giants, no matter what danger lay ahead for him.

The two decided they should embark on their new quest right away and returned to the meadow. They gathered everything that had been prepared for them and were ready in an hour. Juliette accompanied Charlie and the giant to the edge of the trees one last time.

Charlie saw one of Juliette's workers behind Juliette. He cradled a small, white blossom that hadn't opened yet. Juliette released Charlie from a tight embrace and twirled around, scooped the blossom, and rested it in Charlie's upturned hands.

"Speaking of good-bye, I have a gift for you, to wish you well on your journey." She beamed as Charlie peered at the blossom. "It is a Pepper Pixie. It will be of great value to you, but please, be wise with it." She winked at Charlie with a mischievous gleam in her eye. Charlie raised her eyebrows. What did that mean?

She hugged Juliette again and kept the closed blossom close to her body. Then she and the giant turned and walked away toward the City of Dorian.

Chapter 13

"**What** is a Pepper Pixie?" Charlie asked the giant. She had settled onto his shoulder. "I have read about pixies before," she explained. "I had always assumed they were a myth... like a lot of things I have read about." She nudged the giant playfully.

He let out a low chuckle. "I'll tell you what I know. You can decide for yourself once your little friend emerges. They are about the length of your stretched-out hand. They have nearly invisible wings and can fly with incredible speed. Each pixie carries traits that relate to the bloom they are born from.

"For example, a Forget-Me-Not Pixie has an incredible memory and can recall anything they have ever seen or heard; they are most useful as record keepers or messengers. Orchid Pixies are quite delicate, but, if taken care of, are also extremely loyal. Foxglove Pixies can summon the sunshine at any time and can heal a broken heart with a touch of their hand. Rhododendron Pixies have venomous saliva and can render even large animals paralyzed. Pepper Pixies, however, are in a class all of their own."

Charlie looked at the blossom in her lap and touched one of the soft white petals.

The giant continued. "Pepper Pixies are born of the blossom from a spicy pepper plant, and that is carried over into their personalities. All I know is they are said have a 'fiery personality' and a 'wicked hot temper.' It will be interesting to see how that manifests itself in the real thing."

"So, why did Juliette give me one? She said it would be valuable?"

"When an intelligent creature possesses the blossom

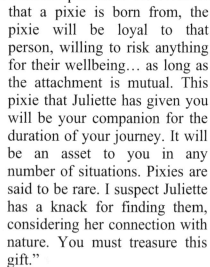

that a pixie is born from, the pixie will be loyal to that person, willing to risk anything for their wellbeing... as long as the attachment is mutual. This pixie that Juliette has given you will be your companion for the duration of your journey. It will be an asset to you in any number of situations. Pixies are said to be rare. I suspect Juliette has a knack for finding them, considering her connection with nature. You must treasure this gift."

Charlie nodded, eyes on the tightly closed blossom. When would it hatch? What would it be like to have a pixie as a companion? Especially one with a terrible temper? She couldn't wait to find out.

It was the next morning that the Pepper Pixie decided to make her appearance. After Charlie had eaten breakfast and she and the giant had begun their walk for the day, Charlie noticed the pepper blossom quiver. She motioned for the giant to watch, and he stood very still as the blossom opened. Curled up inside was a small, human looking creature with iridescent wings wrapped around her tiny body. As her wings unfolded, the pixie stretched, as if awakening from a deep sleep. She opened her large, orange eyes, blinked several slow blinks, and peered at Charlie. Charlie was amazed by the pixie's fiery orange, fly-away hair. She had long, slender arms and legs for her size, and dainty hands and feet. Her face was heart shaped and her eyes were larger in proportion to her face than human eyes. She had very red lips and a small, sharp nose. Her skin was nearly translucent. Charlie was afraid of breaking her.

Charlie spoke to the pixie in a soft voice. "Hello, I'm Charlie. I'm glad to meet you."

The Pepper Pixie gave Charlie a shy grin, and flew close to her face to examine her eyes. To Charlie it seemed that the pixie peered straight into her soul. When she was satisfied with whatever she had been searching for in Charlie, the pixie spoke in a small voice. "Hello, friend. I am glad to meet you."

Charlie rested the now opened blossom in her lap and reached into her pocket for the dress that Juliette had given her for the pixie. It was a simple sheath woven from the soft wool of a lamb. Most of the slender strands were natural creamy white, but there was a strand of orange-dyed wool woven in, which gave the dress a hint of color. The pixie slipped the dress on over her head, and hovered near Charlie's side.

When the giant moved to follow, the pixie darted around Charlie's face. She shouted and pointed at the giant and warned Charlie to watch out and take cover. As quick as a flash, she flew near the giant's face and buzzed around his head like an aggravated insect. In an instant the pixie's skin changed from snowy white to the orange color of her hair and eyes. Her hair turned from fly away orange locks to leaping flames on top of her head.

Charlie called to the pixie with a worried look on her face. "No, pixie, he is my friend! Please, come back, I will explain!"

The pixie flew a few more times in front of the giant's face before she drifted back to Charlie. She glanced repeatedly over her shoulder with a scowl at the giant.

Charlie explained to the pixie that the giant was her friend and told her about the mission they were on to save the giants. The pixie scowled in the giant's direction, giving the impression that she still didn't trust him.

"Well," she said in her tiny voice. She did not look away from the giant. "I don't know. I'm going to keep a close eye on him." The flames on her head disappeared and her hair returned.

Charlie had witnessed the pixie's "fiery personality" almost as soon as she met her. She knew she and the pixie would be able to help each other, but she did feel sad about the pixie's aversion to the giant.

The pixie spent the remainder of the day close to Charlie. She flitted here and there, drank nectar from coral bells and honeysuckles, and sucked juice from goose and elder berries; but she always returned to almost resting on Charlie's shoulder, even though she didn't ever land there.

Charlie told the pixie everything that had happened so far, and expounded further into the mission they were trying to accomplish. She told about her dreams and what led her to helping the giant, and she talked about the giant and what a great friend he had been to her. She hoped to persuade the pixie to trust him.

The pixie still seemed to not like the giant. She often buzzed near his ear or flitted in front of his face to glare at him. It seemed like she was trying to intimidate him, which Charlie found hilarious due to the vast size difference between her two friends.

For the giant's part, he did his best to ignore the pixie. He couldn't hear her words, anyway, and he simply smiled when she flew near him. Charlie could tell he knew the pixie would warm up to him eventually.

The pixie told Charlie that her name was Pepper. "Duh. What else would it be?" Charlie giggled at Pepper's sarcastic attitude. It was so at odds with her tiny body!

It didn't take much to set off her "wicked hot temper," either. The first night they were together, she had already burst into flames three times. The first, when she saw the giant for the first time. The second, when she thought the giant was walking too slow in front of her. And the third, when they settled in for their evening meal.

The giant had gathered some wood for Charlie, as usual, and Charlie had built a small but hot fire. She asked Pepper to light it for her, but the pixie said she couldn't control the flames.

Charlie used her own fire-starting supplies to get it going. She used a stick to roast some large mushrooms she had found. A good-sized wild turkey rotated on a spit she had fashioned over the fire. Pepper found some angelica plants nearby, and Charlie showed her how to crystalize the stems into candy sticks. Pepper was rosy with glee as she munched on her treat.

"She has quite the sweet tooth," the giant commented to Charlie with a grin.

Pepper lit up. "Excuse me?" She flew right in front of his face. Again.

The pixie also did not seem to have any sense of fear.

The giant could not hear Pepper as she laid in on him. She ranted and raved at the audacity he had to comment on the way she ate, the nerve of him making assumptions about her preferences for sweet or not sweet, and the rudeness of talking about her like she wasn't even there. She poked his nose with each point to make sure her message was received.

Charlie relayed the gist of the tirade to the giant, and he offered a sincere apology. Of course he had not been trying to offend the pixie. He only thought it was an interesting contrast for a spicy pepper pixie to enjoy sweet things so much.

Pepper glared at him and snapped, "I'll take the apology, but I don't have to like it." She drifted back toward the fire where Charlie tried to stifle her own laughter. She knew better than to laugh, but it was all too funny. She turned away from Pepper, allowing the shadows from the bright fire to hide her smirk.

Charlie continued to have dreams about the City of Dorian, most short. It was like they were reassuring her that they were headed in the right direction, and that this was the appropriate course to take in their quest to awaken the giants and stop Jessamine. No new information was obtained from the dreams, but Charlie still appreciated having them. It was a relief to know that they were on the right track.

Each day Pepper hovered near Charlie, but frequently darted away to inspect some flowering plant. She told Charlie about the purple sage that was almost as tall as Charlie was. She said the nectar was delicious, but

Charlie thought the pixie smelled kind of different after she ate it.

Charlie asked Pepper one afternoon about her flame.

"It responds to my mood." She studied her fingernails with an air of indifference. "It's not something I can control."

"Do you think you would be able to learn to control it?" Charlie wondered.

"I don't know…" Pepper looked doubtful. "I don't know if I really need to, you know?"

Charlie suggested times where it might be handy to be able to control the flames, like starting the fire each night. Or if they traveled at night, being able to see better.

The pixie was pretty closed off at the idea, though, so Charlie didn't press it.

However, after that conversation, she noticed Pepper talking to herself as she tried to stay out of view of Charlie and the giant. Charlie strained to hear what the pixie was saying.

"Come on, Pepper, you can do it. You CAN control the flame. Just… think about something that ticks you off. Like the giant. And the way he chews his food so loud. Or the way he smiles and seems so happy all the time. Or when he reminds me to stay calm."

Charlie watched. Would she be able to do it? Pepper kept listing things, all about the giant, that made her mad. Her skin changed to a warm orange, but her hair did not light.

Pepper picked up a nearby acorn and threw it as hard as she could at a daisy. It bounced off the flower and dropped to the ground. "Ugh! This is so. Annoying."

Her hair started to glow, just a little.

"It's working!" She zipped upwards. It put out the flame. "I knew this was pointless." She had no idea that Charlie could hear what was going on.

"What is it?" the giant asked Charlie. "What are you looking at?"

"Oh, it's Pepper" Charlie spoke in a low voice, but loud enough that the giant could hear her. She was perched on his shoulder, so she was close to his ear. "She's trying to make herself mad and light her hair on fire."

"Is it working?" the giant wondered.

"No," Charlie said with a sideways frown. "Poor thing."

"Where is she?" He looked around the grassy ground for the pixie.

"Over there." Charlie pointed to where the pixie alternated between a faint glow and no flame at all.

"Hmm." The giant looked thoughtful.

"What are you thinking?" Charlie asked him. Maybe he had an idea for how she could practice.

"Watch this." He stomped his foot, hard, on the ground. The earth shook. The grass trembled. The flowers vibrated. Even the trees shook off some leaves.

Pepper instantly burst into flames.

The giant laughed out loud. Pepper buzzed around his head several times. Her entire body was red and the flames on her head were nearly white with heat.

Charlie grinned. It had worked, but maybe a little too well. "Let's try something different next time. What do you think?"

Pepper was not amused as Charlie and the giant continued to chuckle at her uncontrolled fire. It took quite some time for her to calm down and for the flame to die out.

"Like I said," Pepper announced at last. "Not controllable." Then she hmphed and zipped off toward a patch of buttercups not too far ahead.

"I love her," Charlie said to the giant. "She's awesome."

The giant nodded his agreement.

Chapter 14

Even though she had seen it in dreams for many nights in a row, Charlie was not prepared to see the City of Dorian in person for the first time.

She had been riding on the giant's shoulder most of the day. Late in the afternoon they crested a hill and all at once a sprawling forest stretched out before them. Beyond the forest, Charlie saw the city and the sea. Her heart raced.

The city was huge, enough room for several hundred thousand people. There was just one road that led into the city. It had an enormous, reinforced gate. The wall that encompassed the city was dotted with look-out towers along its expanse. The wall weaved around the towers like a snake. The tallest tower was in the center of the city, and Charlie imagined you could see to the horizon in all directions from that tower. The city was well guarded.

Within the walls Charlie knew from her dreams that there were other brick structures; housing, weapons facilities, shops and store houses, livery stables; and furthest from the gate nearest the sea, the largest building, castle-like, which housed the city leaders. The leaders- who were also the giant slayers.

The thing that surprised Charlie the most was the city's precarious location. It was built upon a cliff that jutted far out over the sea, further than any other point on the shoreline. Charlie assumed they had built the city there for protection. With just one way in or out, any attack would be made from land. But the ground underneath the city was crumbling away, bit by bit, eroded by the wind and waves of the salty sea. It seemed like the whole cliff would collapse under the city at any second.

When Charlie turned around to talk to the giant, she saw fear in his eyes.

"You don't have to do this, Charlie," he said to her.

"I do. For you. And for all the other giants that are still alive. We have to try. There is no turning back. At least, not for me," Charlie affirmed.

Pepper flew near Charlie and looked worried. "Don't do it. Don't do it." She said in her miniscule voice.

"I will. And you will both be here to help me. Together, this is not impossible. Trust me. Juliette would not have suggested this if there was another, safer way to save you. We can figure out a plan. It will work out." Charlie's voice was confident, no trace of fear or apprehension.

The group sat on the side of the hill that faced away from the city. They needed to keep the giant out of sight from any watchmen in the towers. They agreed that the giant should stay hidden, as far away as possible, but still be able to see the city. The giant pointed to a place in the distance at the edge of the forest, on top of a high hill. Charlie would meet him there once she had found the information about the Battle Horn. They also agreed that Pepper would accompany Charlie into the city but stay hidden unless it was necessary for her to reveal herself. Charlie's job would be to find Jessamine and learn whether or not Jessamine was close to finding, or had already found, the Battle Horn. They knew Jessamine could not be trusted and ruled out coming right out and talking about the Battle Horn at all.

Because it was close to dusk, they chose to stay together for the night and part ways in the morning. Charlie did not sleep well. She had several more dreams of the city and Jessamine. At least in the morning she knew exactly where to find Jessamine. Now she had to be convincing as to her purpose for being there.

Jessamine was a trader of valuable goods. A pawnbroker. If Charlie had something that Jessamine wanted, Charlie could catch her interest.

She only had one thing of value: the vial of Deep Spring water that her father had slipped into her bag. She hoped the water would entice Jessamine enough to make their plan work.

By sunrise, Charlie was ready to go. She didn't want to put it off any longer. Charlie's vial of Deep Spring water hung around her neck in plain sight. She made sure Pepper was tucked safely inside her bag. Her nerves were on high alert, and she couldn't wait for this part of their journey to be over. She hoped she could find what she needed right away and be on her way before any other giants were killed.

Charlie's hands shook and heart beat faster than ever before when she turned toward the forest that loomed between herself and her destination. She glanced back at the giant. A pit settled in the bottom of her stomach. She waved a silent good-bye to her friend. Just when she turned back toward the forest, a figure materialized out of the trees.

"Alder!" Charlie cried.

Alder jogged forward and squeezed Charlie's arm with one of his strong, warm hands. "It's good to see you again."

Alder turned toward the giant and waved. He indicated that he would walk with Charlie toward the city.

The giant's posture relaxed as if a weight on his back had been lightened. He nodded a thank you.

Alder turned back to Charlie. "Let's get going!" He sounded so cheerful that Charlie's fears melted away. And it helped that he was kind of cute, too.

Charlie fell into step next to Alder and they headed into the dark edge of the forest toward the city. Pepper peeked out from the pack. Charlie opened her bag and

Pepper zipped out. She twirled in the air to show off for Alder.

Charlie and Alder walked in silence for a few minutes. Pepper hovered just above Charlie's shoulder opposite Alder. "He's cute!" she whispered. Charlie shushed her. The pixie continued to peek at Alder. She giggled and her skin turned a rosy shade of pink.

Charlie glanced sideways at Alder. She noticed he had a calm, confident look on his face. His fingers tickled the ferns and shrubs as he walked by them, and she gasped when she noticed that upon contact with his skin, the plants grew fuller, greener, and blossoms opened where only buds had been before.

Alder looked at Charlie with a grin. "What is it?"

"Your hands! The plants! What…?" she couldn't form a complete sentence.

"The plants do tend to respond to my touch." He grinned.

"But… why?"

"It is my gift, just as Juliette has stewardship over the creatures." Alder continued to graze the plants with his hands, as if he couldn't help being in contact with them all the time.

Charlie looked at the ground as they continued to walk. She wanted to avoid stepping on sharp rocks and branches on the forest floor. Then she noticed Alder's feet. "You're not wearing any shoes!" she cried and looked at him again.

"Nope." He pointed. "Don't need to. See?"

Charlie looked at his feet again. The ground they tread was rocky with sticks and lumps all over, not something most people would want to walk on barefoot. But Charlie watched Alder's feet. When his foot touched the ground, lush green grass sprinkled with tiny forget-me-not flowers sprouted under his foot. They created a soft cushion wherever he stepped. Charlie turned around and looked at the path they had walked, and sure enough, there were patches of green for each of his footsteps.

"That's amazing!" she gushed.

Alder chuckled. "Oh, it's nothing. It's just the forests way of welcoming me. It's quite nice!"

"Yeah! That does sound nice!"

"I know this is all new to you. In fact, you're new to me, as well. I've never met anyone from your home before. Please, tell me about it."

"Ooooh," Pepper's breath tickled Charlie's ear. "He wants to know mooooooore about you…"

Charlie rolled her eyes. Subtly. So Alder wouldn't see. Hopefully he hadn't heard, either.

She was glad to have something to talk about other than the task ahead of her, though. She told him about her father and her home, about her favorite fishing spot and her understanding of the herbs and plants that grew in her garden.

In turn, Alder pointed out to Charlie the names of plants and trees that she wasn't familiar with. Fragrant cypress trees mingled with blackthorn trees. The blackthorns were lush and green, but hidden among the foliage protruded long, black thorns the size of Charlie's arm. Charlie asked about a weird looking tree that had white thorns all over it and was covered in thousands of red ants. He gently pulled her away from it and explained that the bullhorn acacia controls insects. And if one grates the wood into a pot of boiling water, a tea can be made with mild mind control abilities. "It's best to not drink things if you do not know what is in them," he said about the City of Dorian.

Soon, the pair, along with the still giggling and blushing pixie, neared the edge of the forest.

"This is where I take my leave of you, Charlie."

"Wait, what?" Charlie asked too fast. "I mean… you're not coming any further?"

Pepper slumped onto Charlie's shoulder and pouted.

"No, this is as close to the City as I can travel." Alder said with a chuckle.

"Really? You mean, as close as you're allowed to travel or as close as you want to? Is it, like, a safety thing or something?"

"Let me show you…" Alder crouched and held his hand out an arm's length in front of him. When his hand lowered toward the ground, thick, spiky thorns sprang up and he pulled his hand away just before they wrapped around it.

Charlie's eyes widened and her mouth almost fell open before she caught herself.

"I cannot proceed any further. My people's power is too strong for the malevolent magic that comes from the City of Dorian. For us to travel beyond this point would mean our own ruin. The darkness that lingers in this place repels our essence and it attacks."

Alder stood, and they faced each other. Charlie wasn't sure how to part ways with him. It was awkward as she stood there not saying anything. She wracked her brain to think of something to say. She needed to be better at this.

"Charlie," Alder studied her. He had a tender expression. It was like he could read her mind and knew that she was embarrassed and uncomfortable. He took her hand in both of his and gave it a squeeze. "Best of luck to you on your mission. I will place a lookout at the edge of the woods, and someone will be here to escort you back to the giant." He paused and looked deep into her eyes. She felt her face flush. "You are good, Charlie. Remember that."

He let go of her hand and she stood there for a second before she came to her senses. "Thanks for walking with me. I feel better. I guess I'll see you soon?"

"Indeed."

"Um… 'Bye then." Charlie called as she stepped onto the road that led to the City of Dorian.

"I think he likes you!" Pepper pinched Charlie before she climbed back into Charlie's pack.

"Oh, hush." Charlie couldn't think about that right now. She needed to ready herself.

Chapter 15

Charlie walked with steady steps toward the gates of the city. The road was lined on either side with fields of red poppies. It reminded her of green fabric with red polka dots scattered all over. The gateway into the City bustled with activity. People moved in and out with horse drawn carts loaded with all kinds of supplies: produce and livestock headed into the city, while handmade household goods left. Food and souvenir vendors were set up all around the gateway, inside and outside the barrier. They hollered about their wares to anyone who might pay attention. The aroma of cooked meat made Charlie's mouth water. A scuffle broke out as a pot-bellied bearded man accused a young girl dressed in rags of stealing some bread. The child did not appear to have any adults on her side. Charlie so badly wanted to step in for the girl but thought better of drawing too much attention to herself. Besides, it's not like she had any money to pay for the bread anyway. What could she even do for the girl?

One thing was sure: Charlie wouldn't be out of place with all the people going in and out of the City. She'd be able to slip past the busy guards and the crowd gathered around the ruckus.

Charlie made her way through the towering gates, head back as she took in the vast height of the serpentine stone wall. The city was even bigger than she had thought it was from afar. Up close, it was massive. She was glad for the memory of her dreams to guide her, and glad for her small friend in her bag to help her not feel alone. Because of the sheer size of the city, there were many dark, dirty alleyways that resembled the one she had seen, and the streets were so crowded it would be easy to get lost.

She made her way through the crowds. The cobblestone streets and narrow alleys were not just crowded with humans. She saw short people with bushy beards and tools tied to their waists; dwarves. Tall willowy figures conversed with one another and ignored everyone around them. These must be wood nymphs. One dark alley was taken up with what she assumed was some kind of ogre, but she didn't hesitate long enough to find out. A young, shirtless man with wispy whiskers on his chin and furry hoofed legs rushed by, a red scarf draped around his shoulders and a package wrapped in brown paper tucked under one arm.

Was she in a dream? It seemed that way, but, no, this was reality. She pressed on, taking the necessary turns to guide her to Jessamine's shop. The streets were narrow with buildings squeezed in tight on either side. Some leaned heavily, others had additions that hung precariously over the road below. She felt closed in after her travels in the wilderness.

Charlie took a deep breath in front of Jessamine's place. The sign above the door looked like she remembered from her dream: a simple metalwork with three shiny globes that dangled down the center. She pushed through the heavy, wooden door, which triggered a bell to jingle from above. As she entered, she fingered the vial of water that hung in plain sight around her neck.

She took a deep breath. "This has to work," she whispered to herself.

She browsed the shop while she waited for Jessamine to emerge from the back to help her customer.

Many of the items for sale Charlie didn't recognize. A floor-to-ceiling bookcase was filled to overflowing with books, used by the looks of them, that ranged from the size of her palm to heavier than Charlie could certainly lift. Some items, like tridents, maces, and a huge sledgehammer lined with spikes, were dangerous. Or odd, like the jars of various sized animal specimen floating in a cloudy liquid, or weird looking arachnid creatures with large pinchers suspended in a clear solid sphere. Varieties of dried plants that she assumed were herbs hung from the bottom of one shelf. An uneasiness blossomed in Charlie's stomach as she made her way through the shop. What had she gotten herself into?

"Welcome! Can I help you find something?" Jessamine emerged through a tattered, dingy curtain at the back of the room. She flashed a look that held a challenge as she considered Charlie.

"Um, I'm just looking, thanks." Charlie avoided eye contact at first, then reminded herself that she needed to make friends with this woman. She forced herself to look into her eyes.

Charlie had seen Jessamine in her dreams, but this woman was still different than she had expected. She was stunning, and, according to Juliette, her youthful appearance betrayed her true age.

Her dark hair fell to the middle of her back in loose curls, with the front pulled back and held away from her face with some shiny clips. Her brown eyes had flecks of gold in them, and her teeth were very white. She appeared sweet. But her demeanor exuded aggressive confidence. She had a very dominating presence. Charlie shrunk in on herself a little.

Jessamine led Charlie around. She pointed out various items that Charlie may be interested in. "Where are you from? I don't recognize you."

"Oh, um… I'm not from Dorian. The city. I am from… elsewhere?" Charlie's nerves were rattled. She forced herself to remain calm.

"I see. And what brings you to our fair city? Business, family, something else?" Jessamine carried on.

"Well, I am looking for a new way of life. City life. I'm from a small village. The opportunities there are slim." Charlie should have thought of this sooner. Hopefully she'd be able to remember what she told Jessamine.

"You plan to stay, then? Very good!" Jessamine seemed truly pleased with Charlie's fake plan. That's when Charlie noticed Jessamine's eyes flick to the vial around Charlie's neck. The woman gave Charlie a toothy smile. "Maybe I can help you figure things out. Do you know anyone in the city? Perhaps I could help you locate your family?"

Was it her imagination, or was Jessamine poking around for information? Charlie's guard went up, but she reminded herself again that this is what she wanted. She needed Jessamine to help her. "Oh, I don't have anyone here. I've wandered around a bit, getting used to the lay-

out. Do you have any recommendations of where I could stay the night? I don't have much money…"

Jessamine's grin grew wider. Predatory. The smile did not reach her eyes. She slung an arm around Charlie's tense shoulders and steered her towards the back of the shop. "Oh, child, I couldn't send you away and let you stay just anywhere. Some parts of the city are not as safe as others. And you being all alone… it just wouldn't do. Please, stay with me. I have a spare room in the back of my shop, and it is yours for the taking, if you would like." Her voice dripped with sweetness. "I can help you figure out where you want to live, and what you will do to support yourself. It will be wonderful to have a guest!" Jessamine's expression appeared warm, but there was hostility behind it as well.

Even though Charlie's gut screamed not to, she agreed. Jessamine, greedy eyes peeking at Charlie's water vial again, showed Charlie the room in the back of the shop and asked her if she needed anything else. Charlie told Jessamine that she was tired and wanted to rest for a little bit. She sat on the bed that was pushed against the wall opposite the door. She removed her shoes and set her pack on the floor. She stretched back on the scratchy, brown blanket and lumpy, yellowish pillow that were already on the bed. Jessamine said she would be back to wake her when supper was ready.

Charlie sat after Jessamine left. She glanced around the shabby room. The rough wood floor had plenty of open knots filled with grime. The walls and ceiling, cracked and stained, smelled musty. The tiny window near the ceiling had so much dust layered on it, that it let in little light. Charlie made sure the decrepit door was closed, and Jessamine truly gone, before she opened her pack. Pepper flew out and right into Charlie's face. Her body was red and her hair aflame. Charlie leaned away. Pepper had never been mad at Charlie before. This was usually how she behaved with the giant. The pixie waved her hands in fervent gestures and talked so fast that Charlie couldn't understand what she tried to say. She begged the pixie to slow so she could understand her.

When Pepper calmed enough for her hair to stop flickering, she told Charlie about how she saw Jessamine. She explained that she could see people not only the way they appeared, but also based on their character. When Pepper looked at Jessamine, she saw someone with gray, brittle hair and dry lifeless skin. She saw black eyes with heavy, dark lids and purple bags underneath. Her smile showed black, decaying teeth and her mouth spewed green mist when she talked.

"This woman is evil!" Still frantic, Pepper continued, "We can't trust her. Why are you being so calm and unguarded with her? We should get out of here!"

"Pepper, I know Juliette said we can't trust her. But staying here is the best option to get close to her so that we can learn as much as possible about the Battle Horn."

Pepper's hair lit up again.

"I'll make sure I keep my guard up," Charlie promised. She would stay alert and not reveal too much of herself to Jessamine.

Charlie was truthful about her exhaustion, however. She couldn't believe it was late in the day already. Where had the time gone? She soon settled into a fitful sleep. She dreamed about her friend the giant surrounded by giant slayers. He swung his arms in sweeping movements down and around, knocking them over ten at a time. But for every slayer he knocked to the ground, a dozen more appeared, until at last he was overcome by them. Just as his life was about to be taken, he turned his face towards her and whispered something. She couldn't make out what it was. She woke up, the back of her neck damp, and the blanket wet with her sweat.

Charlie panted as she willed herself to calm down. She had no idea if this dream was one of her prophetic dreams, or if it was a reaction to the stresses of the past little while, combined with fear for her friend. She hoped it was her fears playing tricks with her mind. A new sense of urgency washed over her. She had to find out about the Battle Horn and get back to the giant as soon as possible.

When she calmed herself, she noticed Pepper sitting on a shelf, a worried look on her face.

"What's wrong?" the pixie asked.

"I just had a dream about the giant being attacked by a massive army."

The pixies skin darkened to a deep red. Charlie begged her to stay calm and help her figure out a plan to find the information about the Battle Horn. Pepper complied and her skin shifted from red, to orange, to pink, then back to its natural papery-white.

They decided that Charlie would try to get Jessamine away from the shop, and Pepper would stay behind and try to find something that might help them in their search. Charlie knew she couldn't talk to Jessamine about giants or giant-slayers, dark creatures, or anything, because then Jessamine would know that Charlie was up to something. She couldn't reveal what she knew and risk the safety of her friends.

Jessamine returned to Charlie's room not long after, announcing supper just as she said she would. She led Charlie to a small kitchen. A pot steamed on the stove and the scent of cooked potatoes filled the room. Charlie sat at a square table only big enough for two plates, and Jessamine served her a hearty stew of potatoes, cabbage, and some other vegetables that Charlie didn't recognize. She poured Charlie a cup of steaming tea. Charlie sniffed her cup. Alder's warning echoed in her mind.

"This smells delicious. What is it?" she asked Jessamine. She tried to keep her voice even. She didn't want to sound suspicious.

"It is my own special concoction. A little bit of fennel, mullein, and raspberry leaf. It helps soothe aches and can ease anxiety. I drink a little every night."

Charlie took a sip under Jessamine's watchful eye.

Chapter 16

In the days that followed, Charlie worked alongside Jessamine. She helped Jessamine run errands, clean, and run her shop; and Jessamine let her stay in her spare room and eat meals with her without pay. Charlie asked Jessamine many questions about her business. She pretended to be interested in her life as a pawnbroker. They shared pots of Jessamine's tea each night before bed.

While Charlie was out with Jessamine, Pepper rummaged through Jessamine's things. She started with the shop. She flitted here to there, looking for anything that might provide some clues as to whether Jessamine had found the Battle Horn yet. Or anything that could give them an idea of where it would be. Or how they could find it. She became frustrated, however, when she didn't find what she needed. She smashed small things in her fiery fury, then swept away the messes. She confessed the damage to Charlie at the end of each day.

After an entire week of searching, Pepper was downright livid with her inability to find anything of value. Charlie tried to reassure her that they would find something in time, but Pepper huffed and rolled her eyes. They both took advantage of the times when Jessamine was away to search every nook and cranny of the cluttered shop. But the more time Charlie spent with Jessamine, the more her desire for her mission slipped away.

The place they stayed was dark. The two windows that were on the front of the shop were coated with layers of dirt, and dreary curtains shaded them from any natural light. Trinkets and stacks of boxes crowded everywhere, piled in precarious heaps. The places to eat and sleep were tight and cramped. But the people Charlie spent her time with were equally dark on the inside. They were greedy and proud. They cared only for themselves. Or what others thought of them. They had little regard for the well-being of anyone and spoke ill of each other behind their backs. Their main goal appeared to be profiting from anyone around them, at any cost.

Pepper tried to talk to Charlie about her unease with the people she interacted with, but after time Charlie brushed off her concerns. She was convinced she was in a good place. Charlie was not as concerned as Pepper about the risk of slipping into the darkness and being unable to escape.

The days wore on. Charlie asked less and less about Pepper's searches. It was hard for Charlie to remember sometimes what they were supposed to be doing there. Pepper told Charlie they needed to find the information or give up and leave.

Unbeknownst to Charlie, Pepper's searches became more and more frantic. Fortunately, Jessamine was not an organized person, and her shop reflected that quality. She never noticed anything out of place.

Charlie learned later about the events that took place near the end of her stay. Her mind was clouded, and she had not been fully aware of her actions. When she learned the truth, she had been ashamed.

After three weeks in Dorian, Pepper had become extremely annoyed with their situation, frustrated with Charlie's lack of caring, and plain mad about everything. As soon as Charlie and Jessamine had left one day, she had been determined to find what they needed so they could leave. There was one area that she hadn't searched yet: Jessamine's private rooms. Jessamine kept her rooms locked at all times, and the key hung on a ribbon tied around her wrist. She never took it off. Pepper had waited to search Jessamine's room, because she knew it would be difficult to break in. She wasn't thrilled about the idea of possibly getting caught. But the time had come. She had no choice.

She had found a piece of wire as long as her own body, and struggled to fly across the room while carrying it. She jammed it in the key hole and wiggled it around. In her fury, she grew hot, and the heat transferred to the wire. The warm wire began to mold to the shape of the keyhole, and before she knew it, Pepper heard the lock click. She yanked the wire from the keyhole and threw it behind a nearby shelf, then pulled on the handle with all of her strength to unlatch the door. She pushed and panted. Steam rose from her hot body. At last, she had managed to budge the door open far enough to squeeze through the opening.

She flew into the room and dropped to the floor. She had exerted all of her energy to obtain access to Jessamine's room. She had sat and rested, but she knew she must be quick if she wanted to spend any time searching without getting caught.

Pepper rummaged through the shelves and drawers, opened books and flipped through pages, dug through piles of clothing, and didn't come up with anything. She flitted from one place to another. Her search become more frantic the longer it took. After she looked everywhere else in the room, she checked under the bed.

It was dusty and dark under the bed. Pepper's wings had swirled the dust which made her cough and gag. After she flew out to catch her breath, she walked under the bed. She took her time in the dirty darkness. She found a small-for-a-human, worn leather case that wasn't dusty like everything else. She used all of her strength to pull the case from under the bed. She pried the lid open.

Within the case Pepper had seen many things that held value. She found a stack of papers that looked like contracts from other people who had promised to pay Jessamine large sums of money to keep a secret or hide an item. There was a pouch that held some gold coins with funny marks on them, that was so heavy that Pepper almost couldn't move it to look underneath it. She found handwritten notes about places or people Jessamine needed to watch with a careful eye.

After she dug through about half the things in the case, Pepper found an aged looking piece of parchment, rolled up and stuffed in the corner. Pepper took it out and spread it on the hard floor. She dragged some of the coins out to hold the corners. She huffed and puffed by the time she was done. She flew above to get a good look.

It was a map. There were symbols and markings on it, and notes about giants and cities. She could tell Jessamine had put together the pieces she had gleaned from the dark creatures. The words "Battle Horn?" were scrawled in several places. Jessamine hadn't discovered where the Horn was yet. That was all Pepper needed to know. Maybe the giant would be able to use this to help somehow. Either way, Pepper wasn't going to leave this here for Jessamine, that was for sure.

Pepper released the paperweights and the map rolled itself back up with a snap. She made sure everything else was back in the case where it had been, then slammed the lid shut and pushed as hard as she could to slide it back underneath the bed. She swooped and wrapped her tiny arms around the map and lifted it. She had struggled to hold on but had managed to fly with it back to Charlie's room. She stashed it behind an old worn-out ceramic vase on a high shelf and settled near it. She waited for Charlie to come home. She paced back and forth. How long would it take for Charlie and Jessamine to run their errands? But she didn't dare take her eyes off the map for anything.

When the two women returned several hours later, Pepper still had to wait for Jessamine and Charlie to part for the evening before she could risk talking to Charlie about what she had found. The hours had been agony. After dinner Charlie returned to her room and Pepper popped up from the shelf and flew to her as she settled herself into bed.

"Charlie, I need to talk to you about the Battle Horn. I found..." Pepper began.

"Pepper, not now, I'm tired." Charlie responded with a yawn. "Besides, I don't need a horn, anyway." Charlie rolled over and faced the wall. Her back to Pepper, she settled herself in for the night.

"Charlie!" Pepper yelled, although not loud- she was a pixie after all. "Snap out of it! You NEED to hear this! I found Jessamine's map! We can go now. Right now. Tonight!"

Charlie rolled onto her back. Pepper hovered over her.

"Pepper, I'm not going anywhere tonight. I like it here. Jessamine is nice, and there are so many opportunities for me here in Dorian. Did you know that people don't age as fast as normal here? And everyone looks out for one another, always asking questions about each other's lives and if they have seen or done anything interesting lately. I finally have friends that remember things, and it feels good to be part of something so... I don't know, big, for a change."

Pepper looked like she wanted to scream. Flames shot from her head and her skin turned a deep crimson. Charlie couldn't understand why she was getting so mad. She rolled her eyes at her tiny friend.

"Charlie!" Pepper's tiny voice had a lot of force behind it. How was that possible for someone so small? "Wake. Up. Jessamine is not who you think she is. She is tricking you, or controlling you, or, or... or something. Don't you remember what Juliette said? We can't trust her! Come on. I know you know this. Think. Just..."

Before the pixie finished her lecture, Charlie batted her away like an annoying insect. "Whatever. Juliette didn't know what she was talking about. I'm fine, really. I want to go to sleep. Just leave me alone."

Charlie scoffed as the pixie, still aflame, glared at her. Then Pepper zipped to a shelf on the wall and pulled out some rolled-up parchment from behind a knick-knack. Charlie watched as the pixie struggled to strap it to her waist, even though it was twice her length. She should probably help. But she was so tired. Pepper took one last, long look at Charlie. Charlie wanted to say something, but she didn't know what to say, or why Pepper was so upset.

Then, to Charlie's surprise, the pixie flew out the open window.

Chapter 17

Charlie tossed and turned long into the night. She had dreams where her father told her to trust her friends. And of Juliette, the dark creatures, and the giant. But then Jessamine would show up in her dream. She enjoyed the parts with Jessamine. She would speak soothing words to her, and offer her a mug of her warm, delicious tea. The rest of the dreams were upsetting. Her mind pulled and pushed, back and forth, trying to tell her something, but she couldn't figure it out.

In the last dream, Jessamine held a massive basilisk, wrapped around her torso and arm. She invited Charlie to touch it and promised it wouldn't hurt her. Charlie hesitated, but trusted Jessamine, so she reached out to touch the snake. The snake lunged for her and bit her on the arm.

Charlie screamed, the pain red hot. She sat up in bed and squeezed her arm. She screeched from the very real pain.

Pepper was in her face in a flash and glared right into her eyes, daring her to protest. Charlie rubbed her arm and her eyes and focused on the pixie before her. Was this a dream? Or was she waking up from a dream? Was she at home, or in the City of Dorian? How long had she been there? Had Pepper bitten her?

"Pepper..." Charlie whispered, and tears stung her eyes. "What have I done? The giant needs me and I have failed him." She looked away from the pixie. Embarrassed tears rolled down her cheeks. "Is there any hope of finding the Battle Horn now, or is it too late?"

Charlie felt like she had awoken from a stupor. The pixie flew up and gave Charlie a quick kiss on her cheek. She grinned from ear to ear. "Welcome back, Charlie!"

The kiss left a warm, tingly feeling on Charlie's face, and the warmth seeped into her heart. She calmed down and listened as Pepper recounted finding the map, going to the giant, and begging him to help. The conversation with the giant had been tricky. The giant couldn't hear her, so she had tried to pantomime. She had been on fire when she found him, but her flame went out when she had calmed down in his presence. She had been forced to concentrate really hard to light up again, but she had done it! She had been able to pantomime a message, and he said he would take care of it. Then he had sent her back to Charlie. Pepper had no idea what he had planned, but he had promised he would do something.

The events of the night had taken so long, that by the time Charlie was up and dressed and packed, with Pepper tucked away inside her bag, the sun was coming up and Jessamine stirred about the kitchen. Charlie didn't know what she would say to Jessamine about wanting to leave, but hoped she could be vague and tell her she was ready to move on.

Charlie tried to sound cheerful as she greeted Jessamine in the kitchen. A pit filled her stomach, though, and she had no appetite for breakfast.

Jessamine looked up from the bowls of colorless porridge she set on the table, and gave Charlie a confused look when she noticed the pack on her shoulder. She flashed Charlie a quick, wry smile, then left the room for a minute. Where had she gone? It didn't matter. Now was the time to slip away. Charlie headed straight for the door. As she was about to rush through it, Jessamine returned.

The two women bumped into each other, and Jessamine put a hand around Charlie's arm and asked in a sweet voice, "Where are you going?"

"I think it might be time for me to go." Charlie backed away from Jessamine. The woman did not let go. "I appreciate you letting me stay here and everything, but I'm ready to find my own way now."

Jessamine's eyes flashed to Charlie's neck, where it was obvious the vial did not hang now. "But I thought we were friends. Surely you don't want to leave in such a rush."

"I just think I should go…" Charlie wasn't sure what to say. She tried to shake Jessamine's hand off of her arm.

"But I need your help today, you know that. You promised you would help." Her grip tightened.

This didn't feel right anymore. Jessamine's sweetness was fake. Her movements sly.

"I really do need to get going. Thank you again for everything," Charlie stammered and pulled her arm free. She looked around for a way to get past Jessamine and to the front of the shop.

Jessamine slammed the door to the kitchen and whipped around to face Charlie. "You aren't going anywhere." Her voice was hard and her eyes flashed with anger. "You owe me quite a bit for staying here, sleeping in my home and eating my food. You can't just walk away with a 'thanks' and think that's good enough."

Charlie's eyes widened. Her stomach tightened. Her whole body trembled. Jessamine slowly advanced toward her. Charlie backed away until her back bumped into the opposite wall. "But we agreed that my service to you would be in exchange for room and board." Charlie felt small again, like she had when she met the giant.

"That deal is off. If you don't pay me, I'll have you arrested." Jessamine stood taller and tipped her nose into the air.

Charlie didn't have any money, of course. Charlie could see that all of Jessamine's kindness had been fabricated. How could she have been so stupid to trust this conniving woman?

"You lied to me, Charlie. You said you would pay me," Jessamine's voice dripped with fake sweetness, implying that the authorities would believe her tale. Then, in a hard voice, "I will, however, take something besides money for payment. Then you would be free to go."

"I don't have anything else…" Charlie panicked at Jessamine's behavior.

"The vial. You wore a vial around your neck before. I will take that," Jessamine demanded, hand outstretched.

Charlie had left the vial in her bag that morning on purpose. She knew she didn't need it as bait anymore, but she still reached to her neck out of habit.

"That's right, I believe it is valuable, and I will take it as payment."

Charlie tried to make her voice calm, but she wasn't sure she was succeeding. "I… I don't know what you're talking about. I don't have it anymore?" The last sentence sounded more like a question than a statement, and Charlie was sure Jessamine could see straight through her lie.

There was a noise in the shop beyond the kitchen. A triumphant sneer spread across Jessamine's face.

"Give it to me now, or you will be sorry," she demanded. As she spoke, two guards armed with swords and shackles entered through the kitchen door. Their faces were menacing and their postures aggressive.

Charlie was trapped. She lowered her pack to the ground with a shaky hand. She whispered something into it low enough that the others wouldn't be able to hear. She opened the pack. In an instant, all aglow with heat and flame, Pepper raced past Jessamine and the guards in a streak of light. Before they could even register what happened, she was out the open door and gone.

"What was that?" Jessamine wanted to know.

"I... don't know," Charlie acted innocent and hoped Jessamine would believe her.

"Whatever. It doesn't matter. Get the vial," demanded Jessamine. She folded her arms across her chest.

Charlie rummaged around in her bag. She needed to stall for time and figure out what to do. She couldn't give Jessamine the vial.

"I can't find it," Charlie lied. Her hands shook. Her breath came fast. She was starting to feel dizzy. This was not how this was supposed to go. What would the consequences be for her deception? Hopefully Pepper and the giant would come up with a way for her to escape.

"Arrest her," Jessamine commanded the guards, her voice firm as she ordered them across the room.

"No! Please!" Charlie begged as the guards approached.

"This is your choice, Charlie. Enjoy your time in the dungeon or hand over the vial. It shouldn't be that hard for you to understand." Jessamine's stance was defiant and she had no sympathy in her voice.

The guards were in front of Charlie now, and one grabbed her by the arm. Charlie cried out in pain as he roughly turned her around and locked the shackles around her wrists behind her back. Charlie cried. Humiliation, guilt, frustration all engulfed her. What was she going to do?

"Get me the bag," Jessamine commanded.

One of the guards reached for the bag, and Charlie, through her tears, screamed and kicked it across the room. She kicked and pushed with her body. Her wrists were rubbed raw from the tight iron cuffs.

"No!" she cried. "You can't have it. Leave me alone! She lied to me! She's trying to steal from me!" Charlie yelled at the guards as she thrashed in their tight grip on her arms. She could feel bruises form underneath their hands.

"Sorry, sweetheart," one of the guards said. "She pays us. We don't ask questions. You'll be coming with us."

He dragged her across the room. She continued to fight, yell, and cry as they squeezed her arms harder and forced her through the shop.

Chapter 18

Just as the guards pulled Charlie through Jessamine's messy shop, the soldiers in the city towers sounded their alarm. The guards stopped and dropped Charlie to the ground. She hit the side of her face on a table and could feel the blood drip down her cheek. The sound of many loud horns bounced off the buildings and down the city streets. The windows shook and things rattled on the shelves.

"Giants?" the first guard wondered. "I've never heard the alarm sounded before, have you?"

"No, and I've been here for thirty years. Do you think it's real?" the second guard panted as they raced for the door.

Charlie watched them go, forgotten with the new threat. Had the giant come to rescue her? She struggled to get to her knees. Jessamine appeared out of the kitchen and marched to Charlie.

She shouted at her over the alarm. "Don't think this means you're off the hook." The rattling continued. A picture shook free from the wall and crashed to the floor.

Glass scattered all around it. Jessamine looked around in alarm, but continued, "I have your pack and I still have you. Sit tight, when this passes the guards will be..."

Before Jessamine could finish her sentence, the ground shook again, harder this time, and Jessamine lost her balance. She fell to her knees. Charlie nearly fell over, too. Anything not heavy or attached to the walls was destroyed.

The roof of the shop ripped from the walls, lifted by boulder sized hands, and flung away. The walls crumbled, which crushed even more of Jessamine's things. She jumped up and cried out at the destruction around her.

The giant reached and scooped up Charlie with one hand. He bent, face to face with Jessamine, and let out a roar. The force of his breath blasted Jessamine and the contents of her shop against the wall behind her. She dropped to the ground. When the noises subsided, she peeked out from behind her arms. The giant picked up Charlie's bag with two fingers, glared at Jessamine, and took off. The ground shook beneath the city as he made his escape.

The guards on the wall shot arrows at the giant, while others lobbed huge stones. Their feeble attempt had no effect on him. The arrows bounced off his thick skin, and he batted away the stones with his arms. He cupped his hands around Charlie and ran through the city. It was dark inside his hands, but Charlie could hear the commotion as he kicked everything in his path out of the way, elbowed through tall spires, and made his way to the nearest wall. The ground beneath the city crumbled. It swallowed whole sections in massive sinkholes that left debris raining into the sea below. Buildings collapsed, people ran around, trying desperately to escape the sinking, crumbling city. Charlie would hear later that he barreled through the wall with his shoulder and did not slow. He jumped off the cliff to the sea below. A tidal wave engulfed the city and flooded anything that had been left standing.

A trickle of water dripped on Charlie as the giant sank like a rock to the bottom of the sea.

The giant plodded along the bottom of the Dorian Sea. He was instantly surrounded by sea nymphs. Charlie could hear their voices through his tightly cupped hands.

"What are you doing here, giant?"

"The land witch betrayed us long ago. You have no right to be here, land dweller."

Charlie wished she could see what they looked like. She had only read myths about them. Some books said they had the tail of a dolphin. Other stories described them as more fishlike, with webbed hands. They could either hypnotize you with their voice or wanted to eat you. Charlie shuddered. It was probably a good thing she was tucked inside, even though it was pitch black and felt like rain.

"You don't belong here, go away!"

"What's in your hands?"

"Is that a person? You shouldn't bring a person here!"

Their voices were sing-songy, but menacing. Even though her hands were still shackled behind her back, Charlie curled herself into a smaller ball.

"He has a person!"

"Give us the person, giant. The person belongs to us now."

Charlie's heart leapt in her chest. What did they mean? She knew she didn't have to worry about the giant giving her up, but still. She didn't like the way that sounded. Would he be entranced by their voices?

Not too long later, the dripping stopped and Charlie could hear waterfalls as the ocean water cascaded off the giant. He opened his hands, his face close to hers.

Charlie tried to scramble to her feet. She shot him an exasperated look and winced in pain from the gash on her face. Her hands were still pinned behind her back and her shoulders torqued by the strain of the shackles.

"WHAT was that all about?" She lectured him through clenched teeth. "You totally exposed yourself to the GIANT SLAYERS! People who are HUNTING. GIANTS. And now they know where you are! Are you CRAZY?! What were you thinking??" she wiggled more and tried to stand without the use of her arms. She stopped after a few seconds and looked at him one more time. "Well?"

"I didn't have a choice," the giant countered, voice calm as ever.

"Yes, you did! You had a choice! I would have been fine. I would have…" Charlie trailed off. Realization washed over her. Without the giant, she would have been imprisoned for who knows how long.

Charlie ducked her head and mumbled her gratitude.

The giant didn't respond, and Charlie knew he hadn't been able to hear her. So, louder this time, she said, "Thank you… for rescuing me. You were right. You did the right thing."

The giant's expression was sincere, no hint of "I-told-you-so" on his face or in his voice as he said, "You are welcome, Little Dreamer."

Pepper caught up to them and flew circles around Charlie. Her words were a blur as she relayed everything she had seen before, during, and after Charlie's rescue.

The pixie gasped when she noticed the shackles on Charlie's wrists, and without pausing her monologue, shot her fiery hands into the lock of the cuffs and heated them. Charlie winced as the heat penetrated the iron and burned her wrists, but a moment later the cuffs melted and fell away from Charlie's hands. She tried to thank the pixie, but Pepper hadn't stopped talking. Charlie touched her wrists with her fingertips. How long would these wounds take to heal?

At last Pepper ran out of words. She hovered near Charlie's shoulder. "So? What are we going to do now? They know where we are. And they are coming." She pointed across the water.

A huge army marched out of the city. Hundreds of riders pushed their horses as fast as they would go, and thousands of foot soldiers followed at a steady pace. Charlie shivered. This was something she had read about, but never thought she would see for herself.

"There's so many of them," Charlie whispered.

"It's fine, Charlie. We are very far away from them. In order to reach us by land, they will have to travel a great distance," the giant tried to offer some comfort to Charlie.

"Even so," Charlie snapped out of her stupor, "we should get going, and try to figure out what to do next."

They hadn't looked at Pepper's map yet. But they couldn't stay where they were.

Chapter 19

The giant left clear evidence of his path as they traveled as far away from the army as possible. Brush and small trees flattened, and footprints left in soft ground all pointed exactly where they were headed. But, by the end of the day they had put at least a two-day distance between themselves and the army, buying them time to rest and plan.

Pepper and Charlie had looked at the map while they traveled, but it didn't make much sense to Charlie. Once they had stopped for the night, the three friends studied the map together. The giant showed them where they were now and pointed out a few familiar places. Charlie noticed that Pepper's animosity toward the giant had disappeared. His rescue of Charlie must have changed her mind about him. She didn't pester him the entire time they looked at the map together. Charlie's heart warmed.

The giant showed them the wall that surrounded Charlie's home, and the area where they had met Juliette.

He pointed out the City of Dorian and the Dorian Sea. They looked at the notes Jessamine had made, and some of the symbols. Charlie noticed that Jessamine had written "Battle Horn?" near what looked like a mountain range. Pepper explained that this was why she had known to take it back to Charlie.

The map showed a haze behind the wall at Charlie's home, with a question mark. Jessamine did not know what was there. That helped Charlie relax a little.

They discussed the markings on the sea that indicated the dangerous creatures that lurked below: serpents with scaly skin and tall fins, and huge octopus tentacles.

Charlie noticed a cave that had fire pouring out of it. Were dragons real, too?

They talked about what the different markings might mean, and speculated on where the Battle Horn might be located.

The giant gasped and sat up straight, as if he had remembered something.

"What is it?" Charlie asked, surprised at his reaction.

"Just a minute, let me think…" The giant's eyes clouded over as he searched his memory for a hidden piece of information.

"I think I might know where we should go." He hesitated and studied the map again. "Yes, I think it is worth trying."

"Where?" Charlie urged. The suspense was killing her.

"Well," the giant's eyes skimmed the map as he spoke. "These marks here, they indicate a place for giants."

"So," Pepper chimed in, "where are we going?"

"We must travel to the City of Giants." The giant sat back and gazed into the night sky.

"The giants have a city? I thought they were all asleep indefinitely. Would anyone be there?" Charlie was confused.

"It is the home of the giants. It hasn't been inhabited in five hundred years. Its location is not written on any map, and only giants know how to find it. Any human who happened to stumble upon it would not be able to see it; it is well camouflaged. From their perspective, it looks like nothing, easy to pass by."

A whole city that was giant sized? If Charlie had felt small and out of place before, how would she feel there? She kind of couldn't wait to find out.

The trio settled in for the night in a clearing in a small wood of oak and hickory trees. Mountain laurel and dwarf blueberry bushes dotted the perimeter, and aromatic sweet fern circled the tree trunks. Pepper was thrilled to find starflowers nearby, and flitted off for a snack. The plan was to rest so they could get an early start in the morning. Charlie fell asleep as soon as her head touched the ground, her mind and body exhausted from the events of the previous day.

The sound of whispers and movement around their camp stirred Charlie out of sleep in the chilly hours of predawn. She kept her eyes closed as her chest tightened.

They had been found.

How had the army caught up with them so fast? Fear and anger warred in her mind. She would not let them harm her giant friend, no matter the cost. She inched her hand toward the dagger strapped to her ankle, and squinted her eyes open to take in her surroundings.

Charlie shifted so she could see better. Shadows moved around in the trees to her right, and as near as she could tell, the giant rested behind her, to the left.

Charlie let out a shriek at the same time that she jumped and threw her dagger towards the shadows. She grabbed her sling and a fistful of stones from one pouch as she loaded the sling and prepared to defend herself.

She hadn't heard a cry from where she had thrown her dagger, so she must have missed. She lowered into a defensive stance; sling ready for her enemy.

But no one came. They stayed within the shadows and held still so she could no longer see or hear them.

"Hey!" Charlie shouted. "Show yourselves, you cowards! Come fight if you want to take us!"

An old man stepped from the shadows. He wore simple clothing, no armor, and no weapons in sight.

Charlie lowered her sling a little and assumed a less defensive stance.

"I am the loyal subject of Princess Juliette." The man bowed low before Charlie and stood straight again. "My name is Orrin. We became aware of your presence because, well, because of him." He gestured toward the giant, who now stood to his full height, fists clenched at his sides, ready to squash anything that approached Charlie.

"We came to see if we could be of any assistance on your journey," Orrin continued. "Or if you would like us to relay a message to the Princess."

"Oh," said Charlie. She took her time to stand straight and lower her weapon. "Hi."

It took Charlie a minute to calm her heart. She put her sling away and returned the stones to the pouch on her waist. Another man emerged from the trees and returned her dagger, which she replaced in its sheath on her leg.

A few more men materialized from the trees, one of them followed by a red fox, while another had a white owl perched on top of his floppy hat. They were a scraggly bunch, but strong in body and gentle in manner.

Charlie would never admit it to anyone, but she secretly waited for Alder to emerge. He was not among the group, though. She told herself not to be disappointed. She was glad to have some company, even if it wasn't Alder, and maybe words of wisdom, from these men of the woods. She was still a little shaky from having been awoken in such a manner.

The men spent the last hour before dawn foraging acorns, chestnuts, blueberries, and some of the sweet fern leaves for Charlie to make tea. Charlie explained to Orrin, but not in too much detail per the giant's wary glance, which direction they were headed and asked him if he could offer any advice on the best course to take with the least number of obstacles. Orrin pointed them in the direction they should travel and told them to look for a valley ringed by a spiny mountain range. He suggested they head through the pass near the center of the range. He told Charlie it was the only pass for weeks in either direction and would be the quickest way through the mountains.

As dawn approached, Charlie and the giant gathered their supplies and the giant affixed them to his body, oblivious to the extra weight. Charlie stood next to the giant, and Juliette's loyal subjects were gathered before them.

Charlie thanked them for their help. She nodded at each of them.

"Please, no thanks are necessary," Orrin insisted. "It was truly our pleasure. Is there a message you wish us to relay to the Princess?"

"Just tell her of our journey, and that we are still well. I don't want her to worry," Charlie told him.

Orrin nodded; the rest of the men followed suit. Then they disappeared into the morning mist of the forest.

Had that all been a dream? The whole experience had been so surreal. The hour they had spent together had gone by so fast, and they left no evidence they had been there.

Chapter 20

As they headed in the direction that Orrin had suggested, Pepper continued to practice her fire lighting skills. After having been able to control it ever so slightly when she went to get the giant, and then again when she had melted the shackles off of Charlie's wrists, Charlie suggested that she try some more. She perched on the fires that Charlie prepared, and concentrated as hard as she could. Only once was she able to light up, just for a moment, but long enough to start the fire. She was elated! She zipped all around, whooping and hollering. Charlie grinned at her success. And the giant chuckled at the excessive celebration.

On the third day the giant spotted a lake in the distance. They altered their course to fill their water canteens. When they neared the lake, the giant set Charlie down so she could stretch her legs. The giant sat to rest at the edge of the lake, and Charlie gathered the water pouches and headed toward the water.

Charlie inspected her surroundings. The source of the lake was a stream that meandered away through a stand of aspens. The fluffy clouds and blue sky reflected on the surface as if it was a mirror. The lake was twice as long as the giant and about as wide has his height. On the opposite shore Charlie saw some strange looking plants. They were bright green, and were the shape of a smooth clam shell, bigger than herself. On either edge of the "shell" were long, sharp spines, and the place where the spines met the green, there was a red strip. It kind of looked like lips. Charlie shuddered. She would be sure to steer clear of those! They looked like something from a nightmare.

Charlie approached the water and sipped a handful. It was clear and cold. It wasn't as good as the water from home, but much better than the murky water she had consumed in the City of Dorian. She splashed some of the fresh water on her face, and scrubbed her neck. She inspected the wounds on her wrists and used her reflection to check her face. She was pleased to see that they were healing nicely. She would probably end up with a scar on her cheek, but it wouldn't be a large one. The scabs on her wrists were itchy.

She paused for a second to dry off with her shirt before she bent to fill the pouches.

As she dipped the first pouch into the water, she heard what sounded like voices. She looked around but didn't see anyone. The giant rested along the shore nearby with his eyes closed, and Pepper had flown to a patch of clover to munch blossoms.

Charlie leaned toward the water. She jumped when a face emerged out of the lake a few arm lengths from where she knelt.

"Hello," the female voice said. "You should come in for a swim! The water feels so good!" The words she spoke dripped with sweetness. Charlie at once put up her guard after her experience with Jessamine.

"Um, no thanks," she leaned away from the creature.

"Oh, but it feels so good!" the figure said again. She rubbed her arms with the water and smoothed her long, wet white hair.

"Yeah, you said that." Charlie stood and backed a step away. "Who are you?"

"I am Illyria." The woman had a toothy smile. Were her teeth sharp?

"What are you doing in the water?"

"Swimming, of course! You should join me!" she splashed Charlie and giggled.

"Yes, please, come join us," two more figures added as they surfaced. Their own white hair clung to their necks and backs, and their silver eyes seemed too large for their faces. Charlie wasn't sure what these creatures were. She recalled that Juliette had warned her about Jessamine's betrayal of the water animals, and how it had caused a breach of trust between water beings and land dwellers. She backed up even further from the edge of the lake.

One of the figures moved closer and reached out a hand toward Charlie, trying to tempt her into the water. "You won't regret it!" The kindness in her voice was less than authentic.

Charlie shook her head. "No, thank you." But she couldn't take her eyes off these creatures. Their eyes were mesmerizing. They didn't blink. And neither did Charlie.

"But we insist that you come swim with us. You are so young and pretty. It would be a shame if you didn't come play," Illyria said.

Charlie's mind clouded. Maybe a swim would be nice after traveling for so long. The women in the water were very welcoming. She took a step forward. As her foot touched the ground, she shook her head to clear her mind of the hypnotic fog.

She was too close to the water. She backed away. A hand shot out from the water's edge and grabbed her ankle with long fingers. Two more hands snatched Charlie's water pouches and pulled them below the surface, not even causing a ripple. How many of these things were there?

"Hey! Give those back!" Charlie shouted as she struggled to free her ankle from the wet hand that gripped her so hard. Nails like claws dug into her flesh.

She cried out in pain as Illyria and the other two figures that had surfaced disappeared back below the water. Another hand shot out of the lake and dug its long, wet nails into her other ankle. They pulled on her and she was forced to step into the shallow water.

Charlie gasped from pain and fell to the ground. She landed hard on her backside. The hands tugged harder. She thrashed and tried to escape, clawed at the ground and attempted to stop them from pulling her further into the lake. She screamed as the claws only dug deeper and they drew her ever further into the water. In a matter of moments Charlie found herself chest deep in her sitting position. She shrieked and splashed as she tried desperately to free herself.

A large hand wrapped around her entire body from behind and pulled her from the lake. The creatures did not loosen their grips. Her legs burned from the pain of their claws sunk into her flesh. Attached to the claws were two female creatures that had shiny skin and silky white hair. Their legs transformed from one tail to two legs and back again as they climbed Charlie's legs with their claws. Charlie gasped from pain. The creatures gasped for air. After several long seconds they let go of Charlie. They dropped back into the lake and slid below the surface once more.

The water settled at once and the surface was smooth again. Charlie's legs and feet were soaked, and blood seeped from her new wounds. But she was so relieved that the giant had rescued her that she didn't even care. The giant deposited her on the ground, and she collapsed. She tried to calm her breath.

"What were those?" Charlie gasped.

"Naiads. They find sport in luring innocent creatures into the water and drowning them. You were lucky to escape. Few have."

Charlie looked at her friend, whose back was to the lake. "You almost didn't get there in..." But Charlie didn't have a chance to finish her sentence. Three huge tentacles with suckers all down one side hurled out of the water. They wrapped around the giant's ankles and torso and knocked him to the ground.

With great force they dragged the giant into the water. It happened so fast Charlie barely had time to register what happened. The giant struggled and fought to free himself. His fingers left deep gashes in the ground. He tried to slow his descent into the water. But soon his head was the only part of him not in the lake. Huge waves splashed into the air as he twisted and turned to try to free himself.

"NO!" Charlie screamed as she rushed forward to help.

The giant, eyes wide, bellowed, "STOP! Charlie! Come no further!"

Charlie stopped at once but continued to yell. "HELP! Someone, help!" she shouted over and over again.

She watched in horror as the giant was tugged the rest of the way into the lake and the surface broiled and sloshed as he writhed against the creature.

Charlie stood there, speechless. The giant disappeared under the water. The surface settled.

Pepper buzzed over and paused next to her. "What happened??" the pixie exclaimed.

"He... he's gone." Charlie whispered; eyes glued to the water. "He was just pulled under the water, and now he's gone."

Pepper's eyes performed a frantic search across the surface of the lake, though she didn't fly any closer. Neither saw any signs of their large companion. What would they do now?

The naiads resurfaced and smirked at Charlie. They taunted her with splashes. "We got your fri- end. We got your fri-end," they sang to her, and cackled with glee at Charlie's despair.

Suddenly, they sucked in a collective breath and dove back below the surface. A huge tentacle splashed out of the water, followed by the giant's hand clutching his sword. Charlie and Pepper gaped as the giant sliced through the tentacle and stumbled out of the lake. He crawled away from the water, panting, his sword in one hand.

"Hurry," he gasped, "run!"

He stood, regained his balance, and grabbed Charlie with his free hand. Another tentacle found its way to the surface. The giant raced into the trees. He did not pause to look back. Charlie watched from inside his loosely cupped hand as several more tentacles protruded from the lake and a dozen naiads broke the surface. They screamed what she imagined were nasty things at them as they sped away.

The giant raced for a long time. When the lake was far behind them, Charlie said, "I think we are far enough away now..."

"Yes, sorry," the giant panted. He plopped down and attempted to catch his breath.

Pepper flitted around Charlie and inspected her. She did not like the gashes in her legs, but otherwise deemed Charlie safe.

"That was way too close." The giant gaped at Charlie. "Are you well?"

"Yes, I guess. That was awful. I feel sick. I thought you weren't coming back." Charlie's voice shook. She pulled up her torn pant legs to peer at her throbbing wounds. They looked red and angry, and they stung. She poked a tentative finger at one and flinched from the pain. Maybe now would be a good time for the Deep Spring water? But she couldn't. Not yet. There must be another use for it. This hurt, yes, but she would survive. As she inspected her legs, the giant spoke.

"The little bit of the creature that you saw from the surface was nothing compared to the monster that was below. I almost did not escape." The giant replied as he inspected his own body. The enormous, spiked suckers had left deep scrapes and circular bruises all over his skin.

"Here you go!" Pepper had flitted away and now huffed her way back with a large stem of a bright gold flowering plant. "Goldenrod! Tastes alright, I guess, but always makes me feel better. Must have some healing powers or something!"

Charlie thanked the pixie and took the stem. She picked a string of blossoms and opened her mouth.

"Wait! No, don't eat it, silly!" Pepper giggled, hand over her mouth. "Rub it on your scrapes! I mean, you *can* eat it, but it will help your legs heal faster if you just put it right on the wounds."

A little embarrassed, Charlie nodded and rubbed the petals onto her legs. It stung a little at first, but also felt a little better. When she finished, she rolled her pant legs back down, and stood. The giant was ready to lift her onto his shoulder. She grabbed her pack.

"Oh, no! We lost the water pouches." Her voice dropped. Now what would they do?

"As long as we are safe, that's all that matters. People are more important than things, Little Dreamer." The giant tipped Charlie onto his shoulder.

Charlie could only manage a nod as she tried to swallow away the lump in her throat.

"We will stop for drinks when we can, but maybe a small stream next time… what do you think?" He had a glint in his eye and the corners of his mouth twitched.

Charlie grinned at last. "That sounds like a better idea."

Chapter 21

A week later they saw the sharp mountains high in the sky in the distance. They were still two days away, but it sure felt good to be getting closer.

After their incident at the lake, the rest of the week had been fairly uneventful. The giant carried Charlie during the day. They stopped to eat and rest at night. The giant told Charlie stories from the history of his race. Previous to her friend's time, the giants had lived as two separate tribes. However, when a time of war with the ogres had come, the two tribes had agreed to work together. Bonds were made, trade was established, romances blossomed, and the two tribes eventually became one.

One thing Charlie took away from that story was that apparently ogres were real, too. And why not? This place was madness.

The stories also made Charlie wish she knew more about the history of her people. All she could remember was living behind the wall. Mostly alone. With just her father, and no mother. She didn't like to think about it and pushed the thoughts away.

Pepper continued to practice her control over her fire. She wanted to master her fire but did not make much progress. One night, after the campfire died out and the crickets chirped in the night, Pepper hovered over the embers to practice. She squeezed her eyes closed, grunted with frustration, and repeatedly kicked at the ashes in her anger. But she couldn't light up. Charlie rolled over and said, "Pepper, can you burn a little quieter, please?"

That made the pixie mad. She did not like being told what to do. Charlie laughed as the pixie lit up in a flash of flame.

They approached the pass that Orrin had told them about. Once they reached the valley, they would leave the forest behind and trek through the mountains, ready for the next leg of their journey.

As they neared the edge of the forest, Charlie heard a rushing sound from above. The giant paused and turned toward the sound. He picked up Charlie so they could discover the source together. Charlie stood on his shoulder, her hand against his neck for balance, while Pepper zipped up to hover over the giant's head. A flock of birds too numerous to count flew toward them, their bodies darkened the sky from the sun. The noise, however, was too loud for the sounds of birds' wings. As the "birds" flew closer, Charlie couldn't believe how large they were. These were no birds.

"Dragons," whispered Charlie as they landed at the edge of the tree line. She had read about dragons, of course, but never thought the day would come when she would see one in person, let alone hundreds of them milling around her.

The one that stood closest to them bent his scaly neck down before them in what could only be a bow. He lifted his head level with Charlie and the giant, his neck bent in a graceful arch, and folded his enormous wings close to his body.

Charlie was dazzled by his beauty. His blue scales shimmered in the sunlight, and his green eyes looked like glass marbles with a black oblong swirl at the center. The dragon's wings were like leather and matched the blue of his scales. His feet each had enormous black talons, and they shifted and pawed at the ground beneath him.

The dragons parted and an impossibly large snowy owl, taller than Charlie, followed the Princess to the front of the group. Once Juliette arrived, she nodded to the owl, who took to the sky.

Charlie hollered a surprised hello, and the giant knelt to the ground. He helped Charlie climb down so she could greet their friend.

"I am so glad to see that you are well," Juliette reached for Charlie's hands and gave them a quick squeeze.

Juliette stood tall and proud, a look of determination in her eyes as she greeted the giant. She was introduced to Pepper who held her usual hover near Charlie's shoulder.

"I received a message from Orrin that you were headed this way. I know you would not want me to worry, but the news I bring is one that will worry you, I fear." She met Charlie's eyes. "There is danger present, Charlie. The slayers army has anticipated your course and has gathered near the mountain pass, ready to ambush you upon your arrival. But do not fear, for I have gathered my dear friends to assist you." She gestured at the dragons. "They are aware of the risks before them, but due to our close relationship, they have agreed to help." Juliette stopped and allowed time for Charlie to absorb everything.

This was a different Juliette than the one Charlie had spent time with before. Whereas last time she seemed flighty and slightly air-headed; now she stood in command and exuded confidence that demanded respect. No wonder the dragons wanted to help.

Juliette gestured to the dragon that had bowed before the giant. "This is Schard, he is the primary dragon. He will assist you today."

The dragon Schard spoke in a voice that rumbled in Charlie's chest. "We are honored to be of service. While we do not seek out violence, we are prepared to meet our common enemy this day, for any race that would slay giants does not deserve a place in this world. It is to our mutual benefit to face this enemy and destroy them before the breadth of their destruction catches up with our own kind. We hope our defense will provide enough time for you to slip past them and discover a path to your destination."

The giant was speechless. Pepper gasped and covered her mouth with one of her hands. Charlie stared. It took Charlie a moment to process this incredible declaration of allegiance from such a fearsome host. The trouble they were about to walk into must be grave for the dragons to have sent such a large number to fight on their behalf.

"Thank you!" was all Charlie could think to say.

She looked at the giant, then Pepper, then back at the dragon and Juliette. "What do we need to do?" Even though she was overwhelmed to know that there was a vast army that waited to take the giant, the fact that she had an army on her side much more fearsome was even better.

Juliette explained where the giant-slayers army was located. She drew a crude map in the dirt with a long stick. She pointed out several options for routes they could take to avoid capture. They could go around the mountain range, which would take several more weeks, even at the giant's fast pace. This would only allow the army time to either catch up to them, or worse, find the Battle Horn first. They could go back the direction they had come, but that would only take them further away from the Battle Horn and closer to the enemy. Or they could go over the mountains, instead of through the pass. The shortest peak was higher than the clouds.

"The choice is yours. You must make this decision, for the journey is yours to bear." Juliette stepped back to give Charlie, Pepper, and the giant a moment to discuss their options.

"I guess you'll have to choose," Charlie said to the giant, "since you're the one doing all the walking." Guilt pulled at her heart. But she didn't want to ask the giant to do something he did not want to do.

"I will climb," resolved the giant without hesitation.

Pepper's skin turned pink.

"Are you sure?" Charlie stuttered. It was the logical choice, but also the most dangerous. "That is a lot to ask of you. Do you think the time saved will be worth the risk?"

"Yes." The giant had no hesitation in the word. "We have no other choice. We must find the Battle Horn as soon as possible if we have any hope of saving the giants and defeating the slayers army."

"It's settled, then," came Schard's deep voice. Charlie hadn't known he was listening. Dragons must have sharp hearing. "We will meet the slayer's army head on and distract them while you make your way to the range. We will hold them off as long as possible." The dragon turned his massive body and lumbered into the group of dragons. The ground vibrated with each of his steps. He communicated with growls and rumbles to the rest. One by one, they beat their wings, hoisted themselves from the ground, and circled above until they were all airborne.

Worry still tugged at Charlie's heart. "I guess we might as well get started. Are you ready for this?" she asked the giant one last time.

"I am ready."

Juliette gave Charlie a long embrace before she whispered something into the air. The white owl returned with a large, bulky bundle.

"Here is a cloak to keep you warm on your journey, and additional provisions. I understand you lost your water pouches in an unfortunate incident. Fresh, full ones are within, as well as a healing poultice of yarrow and rue, and plenty of dried fruit and mushrooms. Stay safe, Charlie." She turned and indicated for the owl to lift her into the sky once more. Charlie watched Juliette float away toward her home.

The giant helped Charlie take her place on his shoulder. Charlie wrapped the cloak tight around herself and convinced Pepper to settle in her lap.

The giant made long strides towards the opposite side of the valley, and Charlie watched over his shoulder. Schard roared to his army, and they moved as one toward the pass at the center of the valley.

Charlie knew the army waited for her and the giant to come out of the woods. They would not be expecting an attack from the sky. A steady rhythm of air rushed from the dragons' wings as they glided toward the human army. A pit formed in Charlie's stomach. A rush of guilt swept over her for their involvement in today's battle. If the slayers army had weapons to slay giants, surely, they would be a difficult adversary for the dragons to defeat.

Soon the giant had reached the gentle slope at the base of the mountain. They were still under considerable cover as the forest climbed partway up the hillside before thinning. The giant stopped there, and lowered Charlie to the ground.

Charlie had been so focused on the dragons that she hadn't noticed a lone figure emerge from the trees. In the distance, the battle cry from the men as they spotted the dragons in the sky rang across the valley. Screeches from the dragons filled the air. Charlie turned toward the sound and momentarily forgot about the person who approached. All color drained from her face.

Alder reached out and put a hand on her arm.

She jumped, startled by his touch. She put a hand to her heart, closed her eyes, and let out a slow breath to calm herself.

"I have faith in the dragons, Charlie." Alder's hand was still warm and firm on Charlie's arm. "I have faith in the giant. And I have faith in you."

Charlie turned and lowered her gaze. Her eyes stung with tears. "Thank you," she whispered.

Charlie gasped as she found herself wrapped in Alder's arms. She hesitated, then put her own arms around him and leaned into his embrace. It felt so good to be held. It softened her fear and lifted her spirits a little.

Charlie stepped away and looked into Alder's eyes. "Thank you," she said, calmer this time.

"You are very welcome, Charlie. I hope I will see you again." Alder gave her a warm look. Charlie blushed and waved as he disappeared from view again.

The giant slowed his pace as they gained elevation. He told Charlie that he didn't have any experience in climbing mountains, since giants were rarely in a hurry to get anywhere. Charlie offered advice she had learned from her studies. She recommended he didn't try climbing straight up the face of the mountain but make zigzag patterns to ease the elevation gain for as long as possible.

Too soon, however, they emerged from the trees and approached the rocky face of the mountain. From here on out, the giant would have to do his best to climb the near-cliff, hand over hand.

He grabbed hold of rocks. Charlie pointed out places that would be good hand- or footholds. The weight of his heavy body sometimes crumbled the stone beneath him, which startled Charlie. Pepper flew above and tried to holler advice. Before long, after he slipped a few times, the giant grumbled in frustration.

Charlie jumped when he punched the mountainside. She hadn't seen him express so much temper since he had rescued her from Jessamine. Pepper zipped down, hair aglow.

"Sorry," the giant said, sheepishly.

Charlie was about to brush off his apology but stopped herself. Where he had punched the side of the mountain, his arm was anchored. The rocks had cracked open which had given him some purchase.

"No... do it again!" Charlie insisted.

"What??" The giant stammered.

Pepper looked at her like she was crazy.

"Seriously, do it again with your other hand! This may be the best way for a giant to climb a mountain!" She was giddy with the new discovery.

The giant did the same with his other hand and kicked his foot into the mountainside as well. He stood easily on the ledge he had created for himself. He pushed himself up with his legs, punched another hole for one hand, then kicked a hole for his other foot a little higher than the first. It was a slow process, but it gave him much more stability on the mountainside as he climbed.

As the giant did all the hard work, Pepper settled into the deep folds of the cloak in Charlie's lap. The higher they climbed, the colder it became. At the speed they were going, which was very, very slow, Pepper might freeze before they made it to the top.

Charlie shared her concern with Pepper in a low voice, so the giant wouldn't hear.

"I do have some control over my flame," Pepper confessed, embarrassed that she couldn't control her temper as well as she should. "It's not easy when I'm not, you know, mad, but it is possible. It's really hard.

And I don't think I can do it for very long. But I'll do what I can."

Charlie's mind swirled with worries for her tiny friend, her giant friend, the dragons who fought on her behalf, and what the outcome of this whole thing would mean for them all.

Chapter 22

The giant-slayers army lined the width of the valley. The watchmen spotted the dragons and they prepared to fight. The dragons swarmed and attacked in groups of two or three. Wave after wave of fireballs shot from the sky. The fire from the dragons burned through the human armor to scorch the men underneath. The catapults lit up with tall dragon flames that burned on and on. The dragons seared the grass which created huge masses of smoke and choked the soldiers and created limited visibility as they tried to fight back.

The giant-slayers wasted no time and changed tactics. They had expected to subdue a giant, not battle dragons. But it didn't take them long to form a new plan. They launched their catapults into the sky, each armed with huge clusters of arrows. The tips of the arrows were made of the same indestructible metal they used to penetrate the giants' tough skin, and they pierced through the dragons' thick scales with no trouble, dropping several dragons with each shot.

Below the dragons, men dropped just as fast, charred by the immense heat from the dragons' mouths. They were plucked from the ground and dropped from deadly heights.

The battle was fierce. Charlie couldn't believe the sights, sounds, and smells. She had read about battles, studied battle strategy, and practiced- alone- hand to hand combat. But she had no real experience with fighting or death. Her heart broke at the loss of life she witnessed.

The sheer number of men and dragons that died below bombarded her with grief, and after some time she couldn't watch the destruction any longer. She hid her head in her knees. Heavy sobs shook her body.

Pepper stayed close to Charlie. She offered as much comfort as she could, stroked Charlie's hair and warmed her with her touch.

The giant made slow progress up the face of the mountain.

There could be no real victory below. Both armies would be devastated.

Soon the clouds obscured any view of the fiery battle and only offered flashes of light through the mist as fire was shot to and from the ground. The shadows of the dragons that swooped to attack and then retreat were highlighted through the clouds.

Then the cloud cover was too thick to see anything. The cold grew wet. It penetrated Charlie's clothes and skin. Her body shook. She had to fight with herself to stay awake. The thin air and the humidity made the coldness unbearable. Pepper did her best to keep them warm, but her tiny flame was no match for the intensity of the cold. Just before the giant reached the summit,

Pepper passed out from the effort of staying lit for so long. Charlie was delirious and could no longer form coherent thoughts. If the giant did not hurry, both lives could be lost.

When the giant recounted his experience to Charlie later, he told her how he had exerted all the energy he could muster and made the climb over the last stretch to the peak. Once he maneuvered over the top, while trying to keep Charlie secure on his shoulder, he looked down the opposite side of the mountain. It would take way too long to climb down the same way he had climbed up. He opted for a controlled slide down the steep side of the mountain.

He did his best to dig in his heals and press his hands down. He bent his knees to absorb the shock from the bumps on the way down, and tried not to gain too much speed.

Bruised, bloody, and nearly broken by the long descent, he reached the warmer, thicker air about half way down the mountain. He slowed and attempted to crab-crawl the rest of the way. He reached the bottom of the mountainside about thirty minutes later.

The giant set Charlie on the ground, and gathered leaves and moss to make bedding for her. Pepper was tucked into Charlie's hands, and the giant wrapped the insulating padding around both of them, then plopped himself on the ground to wait for them to warm. He leaned against a large boulder, closed his eyes, and cleared his mind so he could rest.

Soon Charlie stretched and climbed through the leaves. She squinted against the bright daylight. She spotted the giant with his eyes closed and face expressionless. She sighed with relief to see that he was safe, and they had made it over the mountains and down the other side in one piece.

She climbed near him to get a better view of her surroundings. The prairie stretched as far as she could see, with clumps of trees and bushes scattered about. She looked to her right and saw the mountain range extend out of sight. Forested land shadowed the base of the mountain along the further reaches. To her left the mountains curved away so she couldn't see the end.

The air was warm and humid. She stood and breathed deep, when she heard a noise in the distance to her right. She squinted at the trees far down the range. Another massive army broke through the trees, their horses and riders emerged first, followed by thousands of foot soldiers. They must have deserted the fight with the dragons when they realized the giant would not approach. They had traveled through the pass that Charlie had expected to traverse.

Charlie shouted in surprise, which startled the giant from his rest.

Charlie's scream also startled Pepper awake. She shot straight up out of the pile of leaves, hair already aflame, and left a smoldering debris pile beneath her.

"They're coming!" Charlie yelled. She jumped from the rocks onto the grassy ground. She bolted to the giant, who scooped her up and ran with Charlie still in his hand.

Pepper flew high into the sky, and then zipped back to Charlie's side. The giant maneuvered Charlie onto his shoulder and grunted with exhaustion and frustration as he ran straight onto the prairie and away from their pursuers.

The giant ran, but because of all the effort he had exerted already, his pace soon slowed. Charlie noticed the difference right away. Would he be able to out-run this army? She looked over her shoulder and breathed a sigh of relief. At his slower pace he was still faster than the lead horsemen. Before long, the men were specks in the distance.

That night, Charlie dreamed of being chased by the army. At first the men rode horses, but slowly the horses morphed into the same evil creatures she had helped capture weeks ago near Juliette's home. The creatures snarled and gained faster and faster. Charlie couldn't run. Her feet were stuck in thick red mud, and she fell to her knees. The army of beasts and men overtook her.

Charlie awoke from her sleep with a start. She slowed her breath the best she could. This had been a dream of fear. Not a vision. She managed to calm down enough to go back to sleep, and she was glad that she did not dream again.

The next morning Charlie woke up as the sun peeked over the horizon. The giant stood and turned in the direction they had come. Pepper was settled nearby, curled up in a moon flower that had gently closed around her as the sun came up.

"The army did not rest during the night. They are catching up. We should leave now." The giant looked at Charlie, frustration wrinkled his features.

Pepper poked her head from the white blossom, and looked past Charlie as she rubbed her eyes. Her eyes widened and she zipped to Charlie's side, ready to flee once more. Charlie took her place on the giant's shoulder, and they were off.

Chapter 23

The giant ran all day and through the night. He only stopped once in the darkness to drink from a river. After he dipped his hands into the water to draw a drink for himself, he warned Charlie to stay away from the water.

"There are dangerous fish here," he explained as he wiped several glowing, sharp-toothed fish off his hand like they were annoying bugs.

Charlie's stomach lurched. She took a couple of steps away from the water. "What are they?"

"Flesh eating fish. They cannot penetrate my skin. It doesn't hurt. Just stay away. I will bring you some water."

He dipped his hands into the water again and allowed the fish to thrash until they fell back into the river. He brought Charlie her drink.

After she saw the nasty creatures, Charlie had lost her desire to drink. She took a drink anyway, only because she knew she needed it.

By morning they had widened the gap between themselves and the army.

The next day, the giant slowed his pace to a walk. The army would not be able to catch up with them. Charlie checked the map a few times, and helped the giant figure out which direction they should travel.

She suggested they rest for the night, and they took shelter in a grove of aspen trees with soft beds of tall grass for Charlie and Pepper to rest on. The heart shaped leaves sounded like a babbling brook as they quaked in the breeze, and the shelter from the night air kept them warm, even without a fire.

The giant told Charlie he was worried he would not be able to resist sleep this night. His energy diminished the further they traveled, and Charlie insisted he needed the rest.

Charlie slept through the night without incident and awoke the next morning when the sunlight warmed their faces. She ran a few laps through the trees to stretch her body and give her a boost for the morning, while Pepper flitted back and forth between patches of clover, sipping the nectar from the blossoms before eating them. The giant stood and stretched as well. It looked like he hadn't needed to worry. He had stayed mostly awake after all.

Charlie climbed back to her place on his shoulder and Pepper flew to rest on her lap. The giant stood and faced the direction they had come.

"What?" Charlie gasped. The army continued to advance. They had gone without rest for the third night in a row. "How can they possibly still be marching?"

"I do not know. But we must hurry." The giant ran again, his pace swift. But within a couple of hours, he slowed. The army continued to proceed at a steady pace, and though Charlie knew the army wouldn't be able to catch up with them, her nerves stayed on edge.

As the day wore on, the distance between the pursuers and the pursued once again widened, but not nearly as far as Charlie would have liked.

The landscape changed as they traveled over the next three days. The prairie gave way to rolling hills covered with low brush and the occasional group of tall evergreens, elder, and cottonwood trees.

On the third morning they couldn't see the army behind them anymore, and Charlie insisted they stop to rest.

"How long will this go on?" Charlie talked to herself. Her eyes scanned the map to ensure they were still headed in the right direction. Neither the giant or Pepper gave any response besides mumbled I don't knows and shrugged shoulders. They were all too weary to wonder.

The group traveled on, tired and quiet, and by early afternoon Charlie saw something loom on the horizon. They crossed over several more hills and through some shallow valleys. When they climbed the last hill that would reveal their destination, the giant stopped at the top so they could survey the view before them.

Charlie had expected to see a city on a hill. But she actually saw a city nestled in a valley. From her spot on the giant's shoulders, she could kind of see some of the details tucked amongst the trees and hills. If she had been on the ground, she wouldn't have known she looked at the outskirts of the largest city in the world. It blended seamlessly with the landscape, using natural protections intermingled with giant-made fortifications. The wall, though taller than the giant, was well camouflaged. The buildings sprawled along the entire valley. Compared with this city, the City of Dorian was nothing.

They made their way down the hill. Pepper whispered, wondering why it was so quiet, and Charlie noticed it was utterly silent.

The quiet, combined with the sheer size of everything, gave Charlie an uneasy feeling.

Once they reached the open gates, they could see by the carving on the stones that this was, indeed, the City of Giants. As if Charlie couldn't already tell.

"This is….. amazing," Charlie's eyes barely blinked as she tried to take it all in.

"Yes, it is," came the giant's awed but sure response.

"You haven't been here before?" Charlie asked, surprised.

"No. Not all giants lived here, or even spent time here. I have never had a reason to travel to this place."

"Wow… This is… amazing!"

The giant chuckled. "You said that already."

Charlie knew they would find the Battle Horn here. The thought of searching this vast area was thrilling and nerve wracking at the same time. Charlie's stomach flipped inside her and her hands shook a little. They were about to find what they had been searching for.

The three friends moved through the city.

"It looks like this place was left in a hurry. What happened?" Charlie asked her rather large friend.

"It is a bit of a mystery to me, as I wasn't here. But I do know some things." The giant talked as they continued to make their way through the city. "Remember what I told you about the curse that caused the giants sleep? When they made the choice to leave the city and fight in the great battle, the city itself was under attack. It is believed that the one who convinced the giants to help also provided a way to awaken them if the need was ever strong enough. The Battle Horn was created as a way to call the giants together."

Was the story true? The giant told it like a legend, and it was so long ago. Would they be able to find it?

The giant carried Charlie down the wide lanes of the city. Both sides of the streets were lined with one-story stone buildings, which were much taller than Charlie's two-story home. Near the edge of the city the buildings were residences, some with small-for-a-giant yards, low stone walls- taller than Charlie but only came up to the giant's knees. Other dwellings were long and narrow, some had pitched roofs and others flat ones. The occasional garden plot was present, though any signs of food being grown were long gone. Weeds had taken over. Many of the structures had vines growing up the walls.

As they moved closer to the center of the city, the residences gave way to workshops, markets, eateries, bookstores, gathering places, and more. Charlie took it all in. It was like a larger-than-life version of her own village. The furniture was gigantic, the tools were massive, and one shop that sold toys had dolls and figures twice as tall as Charlie. She was miniscule in comparison. This place was so surreal.

Chapter 24

After they searched for what felt like forever, they found a room near the center of the city that must have been a storage space. Charlie wandered around. She touched everything within reach. Her eyes roved over each item. The ceiling was at least two giant-stories high. The walls were made from bricks cut from speckled stone that looked like granite, and the floor was tiled with the same material. High windows along the entire perimeter let it in plenty of natural light, illuminating the immense array of items.

Though everything was larger than life, many of the areas had ladders or stairs clearly meant for human sized visitors. Charlie took advantage and climbed as many as she could to take a closer look at the contents of the vast space.

One area of the room had a few tall bookshelves attached to the brick walls, with books of varying thicknesses. There was a pedestal nearby, with one book opened on it and a platform connected to a flight of stairs for a smaller person to be able to see as well. Charlie climbed. She fingered the massive pages but did not recognize the writing within the book. It looked like someone had been studying something, as there were a couple of other books nearby that looked like they could be part of a series or set.

Charlie climbed down and continued around the edge of the room. There were shelves that held what appeared to be artifacts from all different kinds of creatures. Many were large, but plenty were human sized. Several were clearly meant for people even smaller than Charlie. Her hand brushed everything, disturbing a thick layer of dust, as she walked down the rows. Weapons, rolled up parchments, tools, even articles of clothing or armor were carefully organized and grouped. She wished she knew what any of it was. What if something on one of these shelves was what they needed?

In the center of the room was a large worktable with a map spread across the center, held in place by paperweights about the size of the giant's fist. Charlie was a pawn on a playing board as she walked across it. Scattered along the rest of the surface were writing utensils, papers, and instruments that were probably used for navigation or some such purpose.

She climbed down and wandered toward the back of the room and noticed the giant peruse the shelves of artifacts and Pepper eyeing the map now.

"Whoa! Look at this!" Charlie called, and the giant and Pepper joined her on the far side of the room.

Charlie pushed back a curtain that revealed dozens of suits of armor. The thing that Charlie found surprising, though, was the armor was made for humans, not giants.

"Why are these here?" Charlie asked the giant.

"There was a time once when giants and humans fought side by side. These must be the special armor that the giants created for human warriors in time of battle."

"Why would the giants need the humans to aid in battle? It seems like they would be able to handle themselves," Charlie wondered out loud as she studied the nearest set of armor. Her fingers grazed the intricate detail of the breastplate and the unique designs etched on each piece of strong metal.

"I am not entirely certain. There must have been a reason, though it does seem curious."

Charlie continued to admire the armor as the group split apart again to resume their search.

"I just don't see anything that could be what we're looking for," Charlie sighed after they had searched the entire room.

"Nor have I," said the giant.

Pepper rested on Charlie's shoulder and shrugged. "Me either." She had her legs crossed and bounced her foot up and down. She also flickered her flame on and off.

Good for her! She's finally figuring it out. But it wouldn't do them much good at this point in their journey.

The giant leaned against the curtain that Charlie had pulled back to reveal the human armor. He turned his head and glanced at it, then started and stood back. He pulled the curtain closed and studied it.

"What is it?" Charlie asked him. She stood from where she had plopped herself onto the floor.

Pepper flew near the giant's face and looked back and forth from him to the curtain, puzzling out what he could be seeing. She flew back to Charlie. "I have no idea…"

The giant turned to Pepper and Charlie and announced, "It's right here." He pointed to the armor.

"Um… alright… what is right where?" Charlie asked, still confused at his sudden interest in the curtain.

"This part of the tapestry mentions the Battle Horn. And this refers to a legendary device called the Key of Sariah." He pointed at a spot on the curtain.

"Key of Sariah?"

"Yes. It activates the Battle Horn," the giant explained.

"I don't understand what that has to do with the armor."

"The armor is the Key," declared the giant, and pulled the curtain open again. He stepped toward one of the suits of armor and pointed at the arm piece on the left side. "Here."

Charlie stepped forward and looked at the arm piece. "It has markings on it, but so does the rest of the armor. It's just a design, isn't it? Or does it tell where the Key of Sariah is?"

"No. The armor IS the Key of Sariah."

Charlie looked at the giant. Was he crazy? "No, it isn't, it's just armor."

"That is what I thought as well. But the tapestry tells of the history of the human-giant-alliance. It also indicates that the arm piece of the armor has a double purpose. It protects the human who wears it, yes. But it also protects them in another way. It gives the wearer the ability to sound the Horn. To call the giants. To awaken them."

Charlie mulled this over. "That's kind of strange. Why would they do that?"

"It was hidden in plain sight. The designer wanted the humans to be able to call the giants but didn't want it to be limited to one single person. The tapestry shows the designer, see?" the giant pointed at the tapestry again.

Charlie couldn't see from the ground, so the giant lifted her to get a better view.

Charlie studied the part of the tapestry that the giant pointed at. It showed the designer. A woman with long hair the exact same color as Charlie's. She was forging armor. And then there was a completed set. The arm piece glowed. Charlie's eyes continued to wander back to the designer.

"Who was she?" she asked the giant.

The giant studied the tapestry some more. "This says her name was Sariah. She was what the Key was named for. It was her design. It would seem it had been her idea. See her showing her plan to the giants? Here, in the written language of giants, is her name. When the giants fell into their slumber, Sariah was the only human remaining who had any knowledge of the Key. I don't know what happened to her, but the Battle Horn became something of legend, and was soon forgotten by most."

Charlie's heart beat a little faster. Her mother had helped her father in his workshop, from what she was told. She was a metal worker. Her name was Sariah, but she had gone by Sara. Could it be the same person? The coincidence was astounding if it wasn't.

Pepper interrupted Charlie's thoughts. "Jessamine hasn't forgotten. How does she know about the Battle Horn?"

Charlie's attention snapped back to the present.

The giant answered Pepper's question, eyes still roving the tapestry as he looked for more clues. "I do not know. I was overtaken by the deep sleep, as were all giants everywhere. But I was not present when all of this took place. I do not know much more than legend and what's here on the tapestry. The little I do know was shared with me by the giant whose place I took as the guardian of the wall."

Charlie's thoughts returned to their task at hand. Her questions about Sariah could be answered after they had awakened the giants and defeated Jessamine. Her heart beat faster as realization hit her.

"None of that matters now, right? It's here! The Key. There are LOTS of them here. That means we found what we came for! What do we do?" Charlie bounced on the balls of her feet. They would be able to awaken the giants. The giant slayers wouldn't stand a chance bringing them all down. Charlie and her friends would be safe here in the heart of the City of Giants. Their journey was complete. They had done it.

She would go home. Soon! She hadn't known what to expect on this journey, but it was so close to being over. Her eyes stung with tears as she thought of home and embracing her father again.

Her heart felt like it was going to burst. Relief, nervousness, and excitement all crowded in at once. So much had happened in her life since her first dream of trying to get over the wall. What would her life be like when she returned home? But she wasn't the same person she had been before. Would she be able to go back to the life she had barely been living when she had left? Maybe she'd be able to convince her father to leave and explore the vast world around them. And he would be able to answer her questions about her mother.

Chapter 25

"**I** know what we must do," the giant startled Charlie when he spoke.

"Great! Let's do it, now!" Charlie bounced toward the armor. She studied it and fidgeted to remove the arm piece.

The giant hesitated. "There's more to it than what you are thinking…"

"It's a horn, right? Do I pick it up and blow it?" She detached the arm piece from the breast plate of the armor in front of her.

"It's not that simple." The giant took a deep breath and closed his eyes. "We have to take it somewhere."

Charlie froze. "You're kidding, right?"

"No, I am sorry. Our journey is not yet complete." His shoulders sagged and his eyes looked sad.

Charlie choked on her voice. "I don't understand."

"It's not a horn in the sense that you can pick it up and blow it. There is a place called the Valley of the Giants," the giant pointed to a depiction of the valley on the tapestry. "Deep within the valley is where the rest of the Battle Horn is located," his finger traced a trail along the tapestry. "This is just a piece of it, like a key. When this piece is placed in a certain point within the larger contraption, the vibrations from the wind reverberate through the tube, across the valley, and out across the plains. The noise is so loud it shakes the earth. The shaking and pitch of the sound is what awakens the sleeping giants."

"Oh," was all Charlie could muster.

"You sound sad, Charlie," the giant inquired.

"I know, I guess I thought we were done, and the war would be over and I would be going home soon. Not that I don't love being here with you and everything, I was just expecting... I don't know, something else. But if what you are saying is true, it means more traveling, right?"

"That is correct. And the distance is great. And there is a chance we will meet resistance along the way."

Charlie heaved a huge sigh. "Great. More running and fighting and almost dying. I don't know how much more I can take." Charlie's voice broke.

Pepper hugged Charlie tight around the neck, and the giant leaned in close so he could see her face. "Do not fear, Little Dreamer. You will come out of this unharmed."

"Yeah?" Charlie asked, doubtful. "How do you know?"

"I have seen it in a dream."

Charlie's eyes shot to meet the giants. They stung as she tried to hold back tears. "You saw me? In another dream?" A tear slid down her face.

The giant nodded, a comforting expression on his face. "I have. And I promise you, you will be safe."

Charlie took a deep shaky breath. "Thank you," was all she said, but there was so much more meaning in those words.

He nodded in response. "I suggest we rest here for the night and set out in the morning for the Valley of the Giants." He stood and surveyed the room for a place for Charlie to rest. "Here." He spread out a soft fur onto the floor for her bed.

The giant settled near Charlie and leaned against the wall. Pepper gathered her own fluff for a bed as well.

"Thanks," Charlie said. She felt better and managed a smile. "I am exhausted!"

When Charlie woke up and opened her eyes, everything was black. She rubbed her eyes to clear her vision, but nothing. The darkness enveloped her. She kept her eyes open wide and searched for any sign of light.

"Pepper?" she called. Maybe the pixie would light up and she would be able to see again. But there was no response.

"Hello?" she tried again. Where was everyone?

She stood to her full height and hit her head. "Ouch!" She crouched again, rubbing the sore spot. What was happening?

She had the sensation of falling all of the sudden. She reached out to try to steady herself. Her right hand touched a curved wall, and she leaned into it to try to calm the queasiness in her stomach.

She was in a tight space. The sensation of falling stayed. She was alone.

Just when the panic started to rise up her throat, whatever she was in hit the ground, hard. Charlie instantly lost consciousness.

When Charlie came to, her eyes flew open, and she sat up, her breath fast.

Pepper flew near her face. Alarm registered in her expression. "Was it a dream? Did something happen? What did you see?" The pixie peppered her with questions.

Charlie took a deep, steadying breath. "Yeah, I'm good. It... it was just a dream." The realization helped calm her nerves. But then her mind tried to figure out what the dream had meant. Charlie rubbed her temples as she processed it all.

The mood in the room was somber as they each prepared for another long journey. The responsibility of what they were setting out to do weighed heavily on each of them. Charlie knew they could be attacked by the army well before they reached the Valley.

The giant strapped dull metal elbow and knee armor pieces in place, as well as a breastplate that wrapped around to protect his back. Charlie could tell he was not happy about the idea of having to fight, but she knew he would do whatever was necessary to accomplish their goal. He armed himself with weapons from the giant's arsenal: a long, double-edged sword, freshly sharpened, replaced the sword in the sheath at his waist. Attached to the back-plate was a slot for a flail, the long stick tucked in and the chain with spiked ball attached beside it. He loaded several heavy iron balls into a bandolier angled across his chest. He also tucked an extra piece of the Key of Sariah into a pouch that he strapped to his belt.

Charlie struggled to figure out how to wear the human armor. When the giant offered to help, she quietly insisted she could do it herself. If she was going to survive this, she needed to become more independent.

None of it fit her slight frame very well. It was meant for warriors, not petite teenage girls. She wore the pieces that she could. She chose to leave the leg guards and helmet behind and tied the silvery breastplate and lower arm pieces securely where they were supposed to go. She belted a sword around her waist, its weight throwing her slightly off balance.

Pepper found some things in the artifacts area that must have been meant for dwarves or something. She had a leather vest tied around her torso and a sword strapped to her waist that looked more like a toothpick. With her arms folded and hair aglow she came across a little menacing… and a little comical. Charlie hid her grin.

They looked around for water and food sources, since they had used up most of the supplies Juliette had provided. Charlie loaded her pack with any edible plants she could find, as well as the occasional vegetable that had reseeded themselves in the giants' gardens. The giant filled their water pouches, in addition to finding a couple more, and insisted on carrying them in his pouch.

They were cautious as they exited the City. They had no idea if Jessamine had gathered the necessary information to find the City, or if they had been tracked to their current location. The giant stepped out of the gates first. He took a defensive stance and peered in all directions. He shielded Charlie and Pepper with his massive body.

"It's all clear," he announced as he stood straighter and turned around.

Just as Charlie stepped around the gate, an arrow whizzed right past her head and lodged itself into the wooden door behind her with a thud.

Charlie jumped back behind the gate. Her chest heaved and her heart pounded. Pepper immediately burst into flames.

"We've been spotted!" Pepper flew to the giant's face to tell him to come back inside.

The giant took two long steps into the entrance, slammed the gate shut, and secured the cross bar. Dozens of arrows thunked into the wooden gate.

"Charlie! Are you hurt?" He rushed to her side and dropped to his hands and knees to examine her for injuries.

"No." Charlie's back still pressed against the wall. The giant's head dropped as he breathed a sigh of relief.

"But you are!" Pepper said, eyes wide with alarm as she hovered above the giant's shoulder.

"What are you talking about?" The giant looked around as Pepper buzzed around his head.

"There's an arrow sticking out of your neck!" Pepper yelled and pointed.

Charlie screamed and her knees buckled.

"Charlie, please don't pass out. I'm fine! I promise!" The giant reached up and felt the back of his neck until his fingers curled around the arrow shaft. He yanked the arrow out with a squelch. "See?" he showed her the arrow. "Not even a drop of blood."

Charlie's vision blurred. She barely registered what he said. All she could think about was the sight and sound of the arrow being pulled from his flesh. She slid the rest of the way down the wall and flopped onto the ground.

The giant tossed the arrow to the side and brought his face closer to Charlie's. "Deep breaths, Charlie!" He coaxed her to relax with his calm voice.

Charlie tried to steady her breaths, but they only came harder and faster. Everything turned blurry. Her eyes closed. She lost consciousness.

Chapter 26

When her eyes fluttered open, she found herself nestled in one of the giant's large hands. Pepper hovered over her.

"She's awake!" the pixie called. She flew into the giant's face and motioned toward Charlie.

The giant peered down. A look of relief spread across his face.

"What happened?" Charlie sat up and patted her own arms and head. "Did I get hit by one of those arrows?" She didn't feel any injuries but couldn't be sure. She was so confused.

"You are fine. You did not get hurt," the giant said. "You fainted. I have you and you are safe now."

He turned his head to look over his shoulder and Charlie could feel his pace increase.

"What's going on?" Charlie's embarrassment of passing out gave way to fear about what would happen next.

"They are trying to break down the city gate," the giant informed her. She heard a steady rhythm of booms as the men battered the gate with some kind of battering ram. The giant continued. "But do not fear, they will not succeed. We are traveling through the city center to leave by another way."

"There are other ways out of the City of Giants?" What other secrets were hidden in this massive place?

"Some are only accessible to smaller beings, but there is at least one other way out for giants. For just such an emergency," the giant advised. "I just don't know exactly where it is."

Now Charlie noticed that as he jogged through the abandoned city his eyes roamed their surroundings. He was looking for a clue or something.

"Where's Pepper?" Charlie asked. She sat up straighter and searched with her own eyes. The pixie had disappeared since Charlie came to.

"She is helping search for the exit. She'll be back soon, I expect." He didn't sound worried. She probably shouldn't be either, then.

The giant continued his search until Pepper returned to report that she had found it. There was a cave system that created a tunnel through the mountains that made the backdrop for the city. Its entrance was marked, but Pepper didn't know exactly what it said.

The entrance to the cave was enormous, but it was so dark inside. The giant looked at the carvings over the opening and mumbled something to himself. Then he entered the cave. Charlie rode on his shoulder. The cavern stretched high and wide. Huge stalactites pointed down from the ceiling. Equally tall stalagmites reached to touch their counterparts. The air was moist, and the floor and walls of the cave dripped. The sound echoed throughout the darkness.

There were several tunnels that branched off from the main cavern, and the giant seemed to know which one to take. He made his way toward one to his left and ducked for a few steps before he could stand straight again. He moved through the tunnel, which twisted and turned occasionally underneath the mountain. The light faded as they moved along, but Pepper lit her hair aflame as she hovered near Charlie to offer some relief from the blackness.

It took less than an hour for the giant to maneuver through and exit into daylight once more. He knew every turn to take. The writing at the entrance must have given him some directions.

Every little sound they heard, like water dripping from above, or a rock the giant kicked with his feet, echoed for a long time down the tunnels. They startled Charlie every time. Why was she so jumpy? She was safe with the giant. There was no risk of losing their way. She took a deep breath to calm her frazzled nerves.

Relieved when they reached daylight again, she still insisted the giant check more carefully this time for an ambush. Pepper volunteered to check. She flew out and returned in a flash. She called the all-clear.

As they emerged from the dark tunnel, Charlie squinted at the bright daylight. The giant lowered her to the ground. Still on edge, she looked all around at the low bushes and green grass that surrounded them. She couldn't help but expect an attack at any moment. She glared at the clumps of trees and scattered glacier boulders for any sign of movement.

She was going insane. She had to be. She looked at the giant. "Friend, I think we have a problem."

He lifted her to his shoulder. "Yes, Little Dreamer?" he asked.

Charlie heaved a deep sigh, her cheeks burned. "I don't think I can fight." Her shoulders slumped and she looked away from the giant.

"Yes, I can see how that has become a concern," the giant agreed. "Do not worry, we will figure this out together. For now, however, I believe we should be on the move. Just in case. You will ride on my shoulder, where you will be safe."

Charlie nodded. The giant sounded so confident. But she had no idea how this was going to play out. After one minor incident, she was terrified of battle. And she hadn't even been the one to become injured! How was she going to face an entire army when she couldn't handle a couple of invisible attackers?

Chapter 27

The giant walked during this leg of their journey. They had agreed that traveling faster would only bring them to battle sooner, and if he was worn out from running non-stop, he would be less useful in a fight.

The route they took led them gradually away from the base of the high mountains that nestled the City of Giants. The land rolled away from them in tall hills and low valleys. The landscape was covered with nothing but tall grass that waved in the wind like the sea. When they were atop one of the hills, they could see a great distance, but down in the valleys, they could neither see nor be seen. The giant had no trouble climbing each crest, not even breathing heavier than normal. His stamina was amazing! Charlie was worn out just from riding on his shoulder. And from worry for herself and her friends.

Pepper scouted ahead each morning. She zipped ahead and back in a matter of minutes to tell them the coast was clear. Still no sign of trouble.

Charlie asked the giant to teach her to fight. She had spent years pouring over every book in the library back home to learn about defensive fighting, battle strategies, and hand-to-hand combat. She had spent more years after that practicing on the dummies and targets she had built for herself in her father's workshop. She had even set up an obstacle course in the wood near her home. She spent So. Much. Time running drills and practicing maneuvers. She really thought she had mastered all of this.

But facing an actual opponent would be something entirely different from hitting a dummy with a pretend sword. And all the agility in the world couldn't prepare her head and heart for the fact that she would probably end up hurting, and even killing, people. Yes, they would be soldiers. And yes, they had probably killed plenty of people themselves. But how many of them had been conscripted? How many would never have signed up to be in an army? And she would have to defend herself. And the only way to do that against a mortal enemy is to be a mortal enemy. Her stomach heaved at the thought.

The giant wasted no time. He showed Charlie some basic moves she could practice along the way. His techniques were more swift and more accurate than what she had tried to learn from a book. But the armor Charlie wore weighed down on her shoulders. She didn't have the range of motion she was used to, and the sword was too heavy. Every time she tried to practice her defense and attack movements, she was clumsy and uncoordinated. It was so frustrating!

Finally, the giant suggested, "I think you should leave the armor."

"But I'll need it in battle. It's fine, I'll manage," she insisted as she performed another sword thrust and dodge move the giant had shown her.

She looked to see if she had done it right. The giant shook his head, a gleam in his eye. Was he laughing at her? Maybe he was worried about her. But she saw the corner of his mouth twitch.

"I will keep you safe," he insisted. "I believe it would be better to reserve your strength then deal with the armor. You should keep the Key of Sariah, of course, but discard the rest. It will be for the best."

Charlie clenched her jaw. Maybe he thought her weak, but she would prove him wrong. "No, I want to keep wearing it," she said, and continued to practice her blocks.

The giant shrugged but said no more.

Pepper sat on a round stone. Her arms stretched behind her, and one leg bounced off the other. She shouted pointers to Charlie about how to hold the sword, or how to duck or dodge better. Charlie did her best to ignore her tiny friend. What did Pepper know about fighting, anyway? All she had to do was set herself on fire. She could probably burn straight through a person if she wanted to.

After Charlie's panic attack with the arrows in the City of Giants, she had forgotten all about her strange dream of being alone in a tight space in the dark, but as she rode on the giant's shoulder, she recalled it once more.

Her mind turned it over and over during their mid-day meal until she couldn't take it anymore.

"You said I wouldn't die," she blurted out. By the way he jumped she knew she caught the giant off guard.

He set down his food and looked straight at her. "That is true." His voice remained calm.

"But I dreamed about my death. How can that be?"

The giant thought for a moment before he answered. "Dreams are complicated. The dreams like the ones you and I experience from time to time are for our benefit. They don't necessarily predict the future, but they tell us what we need to know so we can accomplish what we are meant to."

That made a little sense. She had dreamed of several different attempts to get beyond the wall of her home. Only one of them had actually come true. But there had to be more to it. "So, if they don't predict the future," she thought out loud, "then I could die, right?" She picked at her prickly pear cactus fruit that Pepper had found earlier.

"Yes. You will die. Someday. Everyone does," was the giant's reply.

"Not my people. They don't die!" Charlie's emotions were all over the place. "They don't even get old!" She didn't want to argue with her dear friend, but she was so confused. She needed to know what this all meant for her.

"That is true. From what we have learned it is a combination of a protective spell and the water that keeps them from aging or injury or death."

"Right. So, like I said, I shouldn't die!" She shoved her food back into her bag. She wasn't hungry anymore.

"Yes," the giant hesitated.

"What?" Charlie insisted. Then sighed. "Sorry, I know this isn't your fault, I just don't understand."

"I will never lie to you, Charlie. I have seen you, and I saw you live. But you haven't had any Deep Spring water for some time. When you are away from your home, the effects will wear off, and you will be able to age, get sick, become injured, or even die."

Charlie threw her hands in the air and groaned. "So now you're saying I am going to die?"

"Yes, Charlie. *Someday*. But not now. Not from this journey. You will be fine. I have seen it. I know."

That didn't make any sense. "So, why did I see myself die in that dream? I only dream about what is going to happen next. And in my dream, I died. How is your dream any surer than mine?"

"Maybe you would die if you hadn't had that dream. Maybe now we can see what may happen and prevent it from happening. Your dreams help you, remember? They don't predict events. They guide you."

Charlie knew what he said was true, but the dream still scared the daylights out of her. She couldn't shake the feeling that something terrible was on the horizon. Besides that, the armor was uncomfortable and it made her irritable.

She changed the subject. "So, have you dreamed about your own death? You say you know I'll be fine, but what about you?"

"Yes, I have seen my death. I am not worried, friend, and you shouldn't be, either." He reassured her.

That was a relief. If they could finish this journey without meeting death, maybe they would be able to awaken the giants. Maybe things would turn out for the best.

"Sorry for getting upset." She stood and slung her pack onto her shoulders. "I do trust you, and your dreams. I guess I'll just have to wait and see what mine meant. What else have you dreamed about?"

The giant lifted Charlie to his shoulder and they continued their conversation as he carried her along. After he told her about some of his dreams, they discussed strategies for facing the army and for taking the Key of Sariah to the Valley of the Giants. Every time Charlie doubted herself, the giant insisted she could handle whatever might come her way.

At the end of the day, Charlie's heart had softened enough that she agreed with the giant about the armor. It was too heavy and awkward for her. If she was careful, she wouldn't need it. She left it behind.

They continued to travel through the night, only resting in the predawn hours where sleep is easy to come by.

Charlie dreamed about Jessamine. She saw Jessamine talk to a man in a dark hood. They were both in shadow, difficult to see. Charlie recognized Jessamine's voice more than her face. She instructed the man to unleash her dark creatures. She gave him a pillow and told him Charlie's scent would be on it, and the beasts would be able to track her. The man opened a cage that held two dozen of the ferocious animals. He had them each drink the smallest sip of water from a clear glass vial, similar to the one Charlie had. He held the pillow under each beast's nose. Snarls escaped from their mouths; drool dripped to the ground. The man released the creatures and they raced out of the City of Dorian.

Charlie sat up. Sweat dripped between her shoulder blades. How long until the creatures found her? What would they do to her when they did?

In the morning Charlie told Pepper and the giant about her dream.

"Since your dreams usually tell a possible future, it is likely that Jessamine hasn't actually released the beasts yet. But she may soon. We have traveled far. I would be surprised if they were able to catch up with us. Do not worry. I won't let them hurt you again. I promise." The giant reassured her with his calmness.

"What about the water that the handler gave them?" Pepper wanted to know. "What was that all about??"

"It's probably Jessamine's supply of Deep Spring water from your home," the giant said. "It would make sense for her to have those animals drink it. Even a few drops would give them renewed strength and added stamina, which would allow them to travel great distances with little rest. It may well be the way she has retained her own youth. But it sounds like her supply is low. We'll stay on the lookout."

The giant agreed, though, when Charlie suggested that maybe she should learn how to defend herself from a beast like that, too.

"You want to keep distance between you and the beast. With Pepper on the lookout, and my height advantage, we should be able to see one coming. But if you were on your own, you want to try to keep it away from you. A spear would be best, but you don't need to be carrying extra weapons." The giant stopped to think. "What other weapons are you good with?"

"I can hit a target with my bow most of the time. And my dad taught me how to shoot a sling." Charlie tried not to sound as nervous as she felt.

"The bow and arrow would be ideal. Faster than a sling. Let's see what you can do."

The giant had Pepper burn a target onto the surface of a rock. He gave Charlie some straight sticks to use, instead of wasting the few arrows she had found in the City of Giants.

Charlie popped a fake arrow onto the string of her bow. She stood perpendicular to the makeshift target. She took a deep breath, relaxed her shoulders, and pulled her hand back toward her ear. Then she released her arrow with a twang and it flew straight into the center of the target. It hit the rock with a thud, then bounced onto the ground.

"Very good, Little Dreamer." The giant sounded impressed.

Charlie's heart swelled in her chest and she stifled a grin.

"If you hear one of those beasts coming, even firing a straight stick at one like that would be enough to stop it in its tracks. You'll be well."

"I can do that, too, you know," Pepper chimed in.

She zipped around and made herself a makeshift bow and used a very tiny stick as her arrow. She landed on Charlie's shoulder to anchor herself.

"Pepper, this really isn't necessary..." Charlie started to say, but the pixie gave her such a dark scowl, that Charlie zipped her lips.

"All right, are you watching?" Pepper checked with Charlie. She turned her head around to confirm that the giant watched as well.

Pepper released her arrow. It shot in a sharp arch and landed on the ground at Charlie's feet.

Pepper rose in the air in a flash of fire, dived to the ground to pick up her arrow, and flew at full speed toward the target. She smashed the now flaming arrow into the rock and it disintegrated in a burst of ashes.

Charlie could not hold back her laughter, which only infuriated Pepper more. She flew around the area as a ball of flame, until the grasses started to catch fire. The giant, also belly laughing, stomped out the flames with one of his massive bare feet.

Pepper zoomed away from them.

"Oh, come on Pepper, come back!" Charlie hollered.

The pixie did not return until much, much later. She had a look on her face that dared them to say anything to her, and neither Charlie nor the giant wanted to press their luck. They kept their mouths firmly closed.

The group traveled for several more days over hills and down into dips in the prairie. They encountered the occasional stream to fill their water pouches. Charlie foraged for parsnips, even though it was a little early for harvest. The leaves gave Charlie an itchy rash. Pepper found some purple prairie clover. She was attracted by the sweet fruity leaves. Charlie found some more prickly pear cactus, as well as some lead plant leaves to make a soothing tea. Pepper liked the nectar from their blue flowers. Charlie also collected ground nuts, wild pearl onions, sunflower seeds, and helianthus tubers to save for later.

Pepper flitted here and there to satisfy her sweet tooth. She found funny, wispy blossoms that looked like smoke. They didn't taste that great. She raved to Charlie about the milkweed nectar. She even chased a rainbow hummingbird from one patch of tall purple cones of blazing star flowers. She announced that she could eat that nectar every day for the rest of her life and never get tired of it.

On the fourth morning, when the shadows were still long, Pepper spotted something in the distance. "Ooh! Maybe it's a herd of golden antlered deer!"

She sped off before Charlie could react. The giant chuckled. "If there were any here, they wouldn't be in a herd. The female elder is the only one with golden antlers, and she stays well hidden. Besides, they would easily outrun Pepper."

"I don't know, I think Pepper can go pretty fast," Charlie countered.

The giant started to explain about the legendary speed of the ceryneian hind, when Pepper buzzed back in a flash.

Alarm turned her skin pink. "It's the army. It looks like it's only part of the army, but there are still a lot of them." She zoomed back and forth. "They are sleeping now except for a few watchmen. You haven't been noticed yet," she gestured toward the giant.

They surveyed the scene around them. They needed to figure out the best plan of action, and fast. Their destination lay in an easterly direction, but that would lead them straight past the soldiers.

"We don't want to engage the army if it can be helped. We still have far to travel before we reach the Valley," the giant announced.

"So, let's take a different route," Charlie suggested.

The giant pondered, and Pepper, impatient as ever, interrupted his thoughts. "It won't be as direct, but we should be able to avoid them by entering that forest over there." She pointed toward a forest of deciduous trees far to the north of the sleeping army, hidden in the shadows of the hills. "There's a large lake the other direction, and we know how *that* turned out last time. Plus, it would be harder to avoid being seen that way since there aren't many trees around the lake."

"Let's go through the forest," Charlie said.

The giant's eyes clouded over and a worried expression pulled his eyebrows down. "I suppose that will be best..." He didn't say more.

"What?" Charlie asked. He had said they should go, but he hadn't moved.

The giant glanced at Charlie and seemed to contemplate whether to say more. "It's nothing."

"What is it?" Charlie asked again.

"Do not be worried, Little Dreamer. All will be well."

But Charlie could sense reservation, even a little fear, in the words that were supposed to reassure her.

Chapter 28

It didn't take the giant long to walk the distance to the edge of the forest, only a couple of hours. Charlie was amazed at how dark the forest was a few steps from the tree line. The daylight did not penetrate the dense forest canopy.

The giant hesitated before he stepped into the forest. The trees were large, although not as big as the ones near Charlie's wall. Still, they were taller than her giant friend and spaced far enough apart that he was able to maneuver through the forest. He trampled smaller shrubs and ferns with every step.

Charlie noticed the giant wince as he paused his stride. He clenched his jaws and took another step forward. His shoulders and face tensed as he continued his march through the trees.

Behind them was utter darkness, as if the forest had engulfed them. Charlie should be able to see where they had entered the forest, but her view in every direction was the same: endless trees, vines, plants, and little to no light. Some of the plant life glowed red. Charlie shuddered.

She strained to see around her, and her eyes went to the forest floor beneath them. She gasped. "Your feet!" she cried.

The giant did not respond.

"Stop! Look at your feet!" she insisted.

"No, Charlie. We must press forward. I will be fine," the giant declared with a grimace.

"But the plants… they look like they are attacking you! They are digging into your feet!"

"Yes, Charlie. This forest is cursed."

"What?! You're kidding, right? Why did you go into a cursed forest?" Charlie's voice was high.

"It was either this or face the army. Our chances of defeating the army are small. We must reach the Valley of the Giants. I can endure much more than you might expect. We will be fine. This is not how I die."

"Can you believe this?" Charlie asked Pepper.

"It's true. I can see the darkness beyond the physical. The plants are malicious. I'm planning on staying very close to you while we travel here." Pepper had fear in her eyes and her skin glowed a faint orange. She stayed very close to the giant's ear and did not stray.

"What are we supposed to do? How are we supposed to travel through a cursed forest and still be fine?" Charlie's voice was a barely controlled loud whisper.

"Giants are somewhat impervious to dark magic. Not to mention that I do have thick skin… and I do not mean that metaphorically," the giant grinned sidelong at Charlie, who did not return his smile. "And keeping quiet is not necessary. The plants don't have ears…"

Charlie rolled her eye. Hard. "So, what? You just plan on strolling through a cursed forest and come out the other side unscathed?"

"Not unscathed, Charlie. Scarred, maybe, but alive. That is something you would not be able to do on your own."

Charlie groaned.

It was hard to keep track of the time since they couldn't see the sun. It felt like they had traveled forever when the giant stopped his march.

"Is something wrong? Why have you stopped?" Charlie asked. She wanted to get through as fast as possible.

"I can go no further." He gestured at his feet.

Thorny vines wrapped around his ankles, snaked up his legs, and entangled him to the spot.

"The forest has halted my progress. I can no longer break free from these vines."

"They're growing faster!" Charlie shrieked. She scrambled to stand on the giant's shoulder.

The vines twisted and wrapped their way up both of the giant's legs. They grew larger and fuller as they spread, and the thorns longer and sharper. They dug into the giant's nearly impenetrable skin. Dark red blood seeped from the places that the thorns stuck.

The giant winced but spoke urgently. "Once they make their way up here, they will impale you. Quick. Climb into my hands. I will protect you. Pepper, take flight, as high as you can. Now!"

Charlie jumped into the giant's open hand. He snapped the other hand over her, like he had done when he carried her into the sea. What little light that shone between his fingers was snuffed. The vines fully engulfed the giant.

She yelled as loud as she could but had no idea if he could hear her. Any sounds were muffled through the thick layer of vines and thorns. The giant couldn't move. Charlie was afraid Pepper would try to help and fly too close and be swallowed up by the vines. She was glad the giant had thought to protect her in his hands. She needed to wait.

Her fears settled. A little. Then, the giant's hands started to press together. It was as if the forest knew she hid in there.

Charlie's breath quickened. She crouched. She tried to make herself as small as possible.

Her mind raced. Was this the dream she had, showing her death? The one the giant told her she could change? She was in a dark, tight space. But what could she do to change her situation?

The giant's hands continued to close in on her. Soon she was lying flat. There was nothing she could do. She closed her eyes tight and clenched her fists and jaw. She waited for the inevitable.

Chapter 29

The giant's hands put pressure on Charlie's outstretched body. This was it. This was her end.

Suddenly, the pressure released. She opened her eyes to see the giant's face close as he breathed a sigh of relief.

"You are not harmed!" he cried.

"How, what…?" Charlie's voice was shrill as she tried to make sense of what had happened. She stood in the giant's palm and looked around. The vines were gone, just like that.

She peered over the edge of the giant's hand to look at the forest floor. Near the giant's feet stood a tree, much smaller than the rest of the forest. But it moved. And talked. Pepper floated near it and talked it's ear off, she was sure.

Wait, did trees have ears? Charlie ran her hands down her face. Here we go again!

The giant lowered her to the ground and squatted to join the conversation.

The tree-person spoke, but Charlie was too distracted to pay attention to its words. From its deep slow voice Charlie gathered it was a male. If trees had gender. He was taller than Charlie. His body resembled a mossy tree trunk with a face carved into the front. Instead of hands he had branches with tiny leaves attached to the two limbs that grew from his sides. Each arm had long lichen that draped down like flowy sleeves. The top of his body was more thin branches with leaves, and she spotted a bird's nest resting there. He had a wooden walking stick grasped in one of his strange hands, and he bent slightly forward, as if he was very old.

Charlie's attention snapped back. She tried to listen.

"I'm so glad I arrived in time," the tree-person said. "I sensed the urgency. I came as fast as I could. I'm afraid I almost didn't make it in time. What are you three doing in this place?" his voice ringed with alarm though the words were slow and steady.

The giant answered. Charlie was still speechless. "We were faced with a difficult decision. This was the best of the options we had before us. I knew what challenges we would face coming here, but I hoped one of your people would get the message before it was too late."

"You are very lucky I arrived in time. This place is not to be treated lightly. It is gravely dangerous. I am still concerned for your well-being. We should begin moving straight away."

Charlie stared. Even though the tree-person gestured for her to follow, she didn't move. Her mouth hung slightly open.

The tree-person looked over his shoulder. He noticed Charlie's confusion, turned and introduced himself. "My name is Gerfott. I am a tree nymph. Charged with protecting the forest. I saw you enter. You seem familiar. Have you traveled this way before?"

Gerfott walked as he spoke which forced Charlie to follow. His steps were slow and frail which matched the manner in which he spoke. Charlie took his arm and assisted him as he walked, earning a polite thank you from him.

"No, I've never been here before," she answered.

"Curious, I could have sworn I've seen you before…" he trailed off. "It was a long time ago, but I can't remember the girl's name."

Charlie noticed he chose his words carefully. Was his memory was failing? Or was he losing his sense of reality a little? She didn't have much experience with elderly.

"How did you find us, anyway?" she finally asked as he led the way through the trees. Pepper hovered nearby. The giant followed close behind.

"I communicate with the flora. I am part of the forest, but separate. I was warned there was trouble here of the, um… larger variety," Gerfott gestured back at the giant with a grin. "This forest is an unkind place to the uninvited visitor." His grin disappeared. "I knew you would be in danger and hoped the giant would keep you safe until I arrived."

"How did the giant know you would come?" Charlie wondered out loud.

"The giants are an old race. He is aware of my presence. I'm not sure he knew I would come. He just took the path he felt was best, and hoped his instincts were right."

Something about Gerfott's words echoed what her father had told her before she left. Her heart twinged of homesickness. She hoped she could follow her instincts as well as the giant had. And as well as her father believed she could.

"How did you get the vines off the giant?" she asked next.

"I instructed the vines that the giant was a friend. They were reluctant to release him from their hold, however."

"Reluctant?" Charlie was surprised. "You mean they didn't want to?"

"That is correct. And they almost did not relent. I cannot command the plants, just give them suggestions. Most flora responds positively to my suggestions, but sometimes it takes convincing. That is why we must be on the move. I'm not sure my influence will last." Gerfott looked concerned as his eyes continuously scanned their surroundings.

Charlie swallowed. She had assumed since a wood nymph had come, they would be protected. It was troubling to think they still weren't safe, even in his presence.

"How long will it take to make it through?" she asked.

Gerfott lowered his mossy eyebrows. She could tell he sensed her nervousness. "It's hard to say. The forest has a way of choosing how long a person stays. We may be able to make it out in several hours, or it may take several days. I am hopeful my presence will lead us toward a prompt exit. We will encounter more difficulties before we make it all the way out, I suspect."

Gerfott led them through the forest into what must have been late afternoon; it was difficult to gauge the exact time. He often grew quiet as he gathered information from the plants. Other times, he carried on casual conversation with Charlie and the giant. Pepper flew above them, also on the look-out for danger.

What little light that reached them through the canopy faded fast.

"Something is coming," Gerfott spoke suddenly.

Charlie looked around. "Where?"

"From that direction." He pointed to their left.

As he said this, Charlie could hear a crashing sound through the thick trees and brush. "What is it?" she asked, fear washed over her again.

"I am not certain. But it is moving quickly. There aren't usually animals in this forest, the vegetation does not allow it. We must move away from here." He relayed his message to the giant, then led them away from the oncoming threat.

Charlie followed Gerfott closely but peeked over her shoulder just as five of Jessamine's dark creatures burst through the underbrush.

Charlie screamed. "Run!"

"This way, hurry!" Gerfott called. He guided them to a grove of trees topped with enormous sparkling golden blossoms. The giant's broad shoulders brushed the blossoms as they ran through the grove.

A glittery golden powder descended from the canopy above them. Charlie was about to ask Gerfott what it was when Pepper dropped from the sky, bounced off the giant's shoulder, and landed on the ground at Charlie's feet.

Charlie let out a startled cry and scooped up the tiny pixie as they continued to run.

"Gerfott, what happened?" Tears pricked her eyes at the sight of her small friend limp in her hands.

"We must keep moving, those beasts are catching up," was all the wood nymph said.

"I can carry you," the giant lowered his hand to the forest floor, but Gerfott had already moved away from him.

"No," Gerfott said. "It is better for me to stay in contact with the forest."

Charlie cradled Pepper in her hand as she jogged along beside Gerfott, while the giant had no trouble keeping pace close behind.

Charlie's pace slowed; her body weighed down with fatigue. "I need to rest," she called to Gerfott. She already lagged behind.

Gerfott turned around, alarm covered his wooden face. "No, we must keep moving." His voice was commanding.

"But I'm so tired, I need to rest." A yawn escaped her mouth as she spoke.

Gerfott hurried back to Charlie and pulled her along while he continued his quick pace.

"What's happening?" the giant asked Gerfott.

"It's the pollen. It causes anyone who inhales it to fall into a deep sleep. The only way to awaken from the sleep is to escape the pollen. But obviously you would not be able to escape if you are asleep. You see the trap."

"Why is it not affecting you and I?" the giant asked. He glanced back when the first of the dark creatures tumbled to the ground, unconscious.

"I am immune to it, and I suspect you just haven't inhaled enough quantity for it to have effect on your rather large physique. I'm not sure how much longer Charlie will last, though."

"Let me take her," the giant insisted. He extended his hand down. Charlie didn't know what they talked about. Her eyelids drooped as she took increasingly clumsy steps.

Gerfott guided her to the giant's hand, and she stumbled onto it, then collapsed. The giant cupped his hand and straightened tall again. The giant followed Gerfott as he maneuvered them through the grove.

By the time they made it out, all five of the dark creatures had succumbed to the pollen and were in a permanent sleep.

Once they were sure they were clear of the threat, Gerfott told the giant it would be safe to stop.

"Charlie should recover within a few minutes. It may take longer for the pixie. She is so tiny." Gerfott explained.

The giant kneeled to the ground and lowered Charlie so Gerfott could see the sleeping pair. Just as he had said, Charlie stirred within a few minutes. She sat up and rubbed her eyes.

Her voice was thick with grogginess as she asked for an explanation.

"It's fine, Charlie. You are safe," the giant assured her. He let out a long sigh of relief.

Charlie looked into her own hands, remembering that Pepper had been there the last time she had been awake.

"Where's Pepper?" she asked when she realized the pixie was no longer there. She spotted her also resting on the giant's hand. "Oh, no! She's not... she'll be fine, right?"

"Yes, she'll be fine, too. She just needs more time to recover," the giant explained.

Gerfott gave Charlie a brief explanation of how the pollen affected them, and told Charlie how they had managed to escape, and how the dark creatures had not.

"We should get moving," Gerfott said once more. "There are more of those beasts in the forest."

Chapter 30

Pepper awoke as they entered a different part of the forest. She stretched her wings and listened to the story of their escape from the dark creatures.

The part of the forest they walked into was full of colorful blossoms that grew low, close to the forest floor. Everything around them bloomed.

"This is amazing!" Charlie said as she reached out her hand to touch one of the nearby flowers.

"Stop!" Gerfott cried. He grabbed her hand before she could touch the flower. "These flowers are carnivorous," he explained.

"What?! Is nothing in this forest normal?" Charlie asked.

"Actually, no," Gerfott shrugged. The bark on his face turned up a little.

She rolled her eyes. "Figures."

"What do you mean?" Gerfott inquired.

Charlie was careful to avoid touching the deadly flowers as they made their way through the garden.
"It seems like we just have one bad thing happen after another. Just when I think things can't get any worse, they do. It would be nice to have something go right for a change, that's all."

"All will be well, Charlie." Gerfott reassured her. "The good thing about facing a trial is the growth your character goes through by the time you have overcome. We all turn into better versions of ourselves when we face challenges. A tree that grows in a windy place has stronger, deeper roots and is more resilient than one that grows in a tranquil setting. One day you'll look back on

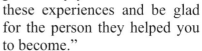

these experiences and be glad for the person they helped you to become."

Just then, the giant, who walked behind them said, "Uh, oh!"

Charlie and Gerfott turned to see the giant with a guilty look on his face. A swarm of thousands of bees buzzed up from the ground where their hive had been knocked over.

Charlie couldn't believe how many bees there were. Way more than should have fit inside the hive at the giant's feet. They buzzed out of the hive so fast, and surrounded the giant before they made their way towards Charlie and Gerfott.

"Quick!" Gerfott yelled as he pulled Charlie close to him and bent low to the ground. He leaned on his walking stick for balance. Charlie crouched beside him. He placed his hand on the ground. Leafy vines shot out of the ground and wrapped all around Gerfott and Charlie without touching them. Charlie threw her arms over her head. The vines formed a shelter around her and Gerfott, and she could hear the buzzing get louder as the bees encircled the pair. The ground shook as the giant yelled and stomped. He must be swatting the bees away from him.

"Where's Pepper?" Gerfott whispered to Charlie.

"She was flying near the giant last I checked, I'm sure she was able to out fly the bees. She's pretty fast," Charlie explained.

"Good, these bees are extremely deadly..."

"Like everything else here, right?" Charlie finished.

Gerfott chuckled, though he still looked concerned. "Yes, like everything else in this forest. Except me, of course. We should be safe within these vines, but it may take some time for the bees to disperse. Are you comfortable?"

"Yeah, I'm good."

"All we can do is wait."

Charlie nodded, and the two fell into silence as they waited for the bees to disperse.

They could hear the giant fight with the bees for what seemed like hours before he tapped the top of Gerfott's vine-cocoon.

"All clear," he said.

Gerfott lifted his hand from the ground and the vines withered away. They tickled as they slid down Charlie's arms and legs.

"Ooh, I'm a little stiff," Gerfott shook out his arms and legs. Leaves floated to the ground.

"Sorry," the giant apologized to the pair. "I must have bumped the hive from a tree, and it detached and crashed to the ground."

"Are you hurt?" Charlie asked. She scanned the giant with her eyes.

"A few stings, but they don't hurt. Thick skin, remember?" the giant answered.

"Right. Any sign of Pepper?"

"No…" he looked around.

"She'll find her way back, I'm sure," Gerfott said.

The group moved forward again, and sure enough, Pepper showed up before long. Her skin glowed dark pink, and she had a sheepish look on her face.

"Um, Pepper?" Charlie's eyes were full of questions.

Pepper ducked her head and avoided eye contact. She hovered near Charlie. "The bees were my fault. Sorry," she said quietly.

"He thought he bumped the hive…" Charlie pointed over her shoulder at the giant.

"Maybe, but I was the one that loosened it from the tree. I really wanted some of the honey, and I poked it with a stick a few times to see if I could get some. They didn't seem bothered by me. I guess I'm too small to be considered a threat. But it was fun watching the hive swing back and forth, so I kept on nudging it. I could tell it was starting to come loose, but I thought it would hold." Pepper talked faster than a bee buzzes. "The giant must have bumped the tree when he walked by, and the hive broke free of its branch. If I had known that would happen, or if I had known you guys would have been in danger, I never would have done it, I promise!"

"Everyone is safe, and it was an accident. Do not be too hard on yourself," Gerfott joined the conversation.

"I know, but I love Charlie and would never do anything to hurt her. I feel terrible. I'm so sorry," Pepper's blush grew darker.

Charlie grinned. "It's fine, Pepper. I forgive you."

The pixie's skin paled once more. "Thanks!" and she zipped around Charlie a few times before she settled on her shoulder. "Maybe I'll stay here for a while, to keep myself out of trouble."

"That sounds smart," Charlie acknowledged. She continued to follow Gerfott through the forest. Pepper licked the honey off her fingers with a satisfied grin.

It didn't take long for Gerfott to announce that the edge of the forest was near. Charlie was relieved that they would more or less be safe again.

When they emerged, Charlie was surprised to see it was morning.

"We must have walked all night!" She shielded her eyes form the morning sun. "No wonder my feet are so tired! I'm glad it's daytime, the sun feels so good!" She took a deep breath, closed her eyes, and leaned her head back to soak in the warmth.

"Thank you, Gerfott, for your assistance," the giant told the wood nymph.

"You are most welcome." He turned to Charlie. "You still have quite a journey ahead of you. I hope you will remain safe. Listen to your heart as you face difficult decisions. Stay close to the giant."

Charlie watched as he slowly made his way back into the trees.

"Good-bye," she whispered. The wood nymph disappeared into the darkness, as if he had turned into one of the trees himself.

Chapter 31

The giant continued to work with Charlie on her fighting skills. He taught her a series of maneuvers and explained that if she practiced enough, she would form muscle memory. She wouldn't have to think about what to do, her body would react instinctively. She also had to unlearn some of the less effective moves that she had practiced years before. She spent every morning, lunch time, and evening practicing until her muscles were no longer sore. Her speed and accuracy increased. The giant was satisfied that she would be fine in a battle. Charlie hoped he was right. And also, that maybe, she wouldn't have to find out.

A week later they were close enough to the dual mountains that they had a clear view of the prairie that the mountains stood over.

Below the peaks they could see a dark shadow that danced on the ground far in the distance. After focusing on the shadow, the trio acknowledged that the army of giant-slayers awaited them at the very end of their journey.

Jessamine must have gained information as to the whereabouts of the Valley of the Giants. She had amassed a huge army- bigger than the ones the three had encountered before. Charlie was aware that they would not receive any help like they had before- from dragon, human, or otherwise. They stopped far enough away that they had not been spotted by the army. The three friends gathered together to devise a plan of action.

Down the prairie, the low mountains stretched out form either side of the two peaks as far as the eye could see. They could tell there was a deep rift in the ground that separated the prairie from the mountainsides, as if the mountain had torn itself away from the land before it. That ruled out an easy passage to the two peaks. They would have to engage the army in order to cross the ravine and climb one of the mountains to the valley that lay nestled behind.

The responsibility that lay on her shoulders was overwhelming. Charlie was quiet as she pondered their next move. If they fought, they would be overcome. They couldn't sneak. Pepper couldn't fly the Key over; it was too big and heavy. There wasn't a solution that didn't involve fighting, or one of them getting hurt. Or worse.

Defeat washed over Charlie.

The giant broke the silence in a somber voice that reflected her anxiety. "I have an idea that will get you across the gorge," started the giant. "I can run into the army and then…"

"No," Charlie interrupted. There were hundreds of thousands of soldiers in front of them. The giant wouldn't stand a chance among them, even with his tough skin and body armor. She would not risk his safety like that.

"No," she said again. "I will sneak in and assess the situation. I'll try to find some kind of weakness or something that will help us get across."

"That is not acceptable." The giant asserted. "You are one person against thousands. You wouldn't survive."

"But they would see you coming!" she countered. "They would start attacking you before you even got close enough to look them in the eye!"

The two argued in muted tones for several minutes before Pepper burst into flames between them. It startled them both into silence. "Stop! Neither of you would make it very far. I can fly right over them and they won't even know I'm there. I'll be back in a sec." And without giving either of them a chance to protest, she flew away.

When she returned a few short minutes later, she reported what she had seen.

"They haven't seen you yet," she said to the giant. "They are just milling about, talking and practicing their fighting. The men closer to the ravine are trying to construct a bridge across. They aren't having much success... idiots." She rolled her eyes.

She told them that there was no other way across the gorge as far as the eye could see. She had seen snarling dark beasts locating and marking sleeping giants here and there. The men that had followed the beasts had begun constructing the killing devices over several of the sleeping giants. She had crossed the ravine and spotted a group of about twenty soldiers hiking on the mountain. They were headed towards the hidden valley where the Battle Horn rested. Though, Pepper didn't know if they knew that it was even there.

At that point, she had zipped back to Charlie and the giant.

"There's no way to cross the ravine without engaging the army," she concluded.

"We need to do something, now." Charlie demanded. Fear and anger mingled in her heart and she needed to end this. "There's no time to spare if we are going to save the giants and stop Jessamine."

The giant nodded. "I know. Like I said, I have an idea. Let me show you what I found in the armory at the City of Giants."

He pulled one of the metal balls out of the bandolier slung across his chest and shoulder. He rested it in the palm of his outstretched hand. "These were something that the giants used in battle when we fought alongside humans."

The giant pressed on the side of the ball, and it bisected into two halves connected by a hinge. "A person would climb inside and the giant would close the ball and throw it high into the air above the opposing army. The person inside would press a release and a parachute would engage, allowing the ball to float to the ground. Upon impact the ball would spring open and the soldier inside would attack from behind enemy lines, confusing the enemy and giving our side an advantage. It was also used at night to allow spies to float into enemy fortresses without being noticed."

The giant snapped the ball shut and set it in front of Charlie. It was twice as tall as she was. She would easily fit inside. Pepper zipped around the circumference, inspecting its workmanship.

"This is pretty cool," she admitted.

The giant nodded. "We can use this ball to get you to the other side of the gorge. You wouldn't have to face the army. You would be safe."

Charlie stared at him, mouth agape. "You want me to get in that thing? Are you serious? It would be dark and I would be alone, flying through the air, right? Um, no. Not after the dream I had. No way!" she crossed her arms. "Besides, it would be way too dangerous for you. It's not like you can take on an entire army alone. There has to be another way."

"We talked about your dream. You will be safe, I promise. You have to trust me. We can think of a way to make this work," the giant responded. He would not give up on his crazy idea.

"So? Even if I was safe, you wouldn't be!" she insisted.

"I also told you that I am not worried about myself."

"I know… this is all just so impossible. We're stuck," Charlie threw her hands up in defeat.

"It is not impossible. If we work together, and trust in what we know, it will be fine," the giant said with confidence.

Pepper nodded her agreement. "We'll figure it out!"

"Fine, say I agreed to this plan… which I don't! What if the parachute doesn't engage? I dreamed about falling and impacting hard enough to kill me. How am I going to do this without dying?" she let her skepticism seep into her words.

"You saw this in a dream, and it didn't end well. Is there something that can be done different to prevent that outcome?" the giant asked.

They thought over the dilemma for a few minutes when Pepper chimed in, "What about the water?"

"What do you mean?" asked Charlie.

"Doesn't your water have, like, magical powers, or something?" Pepper reminded them.

"It does," the giant nodded. "Healing power."

Pepper continued her thought as she flew back and forth between Charlie and the giant. She gestured wildly as she spoke. "The water would protect you. If you drink it the moment the ball impacts with the ground, it will heal any injuries you may sustain... even life-threatening ones."

Charlie thought through the logistics. "I guess that could work... But it's still pretty scary. What if I don't drink it in time? Or it doesn't work? Or..."

The giant interrupted with his deep, calm voice, "It will work, Charlie."

She took a deep breath. She mulled over this idea. She had always leaned on herself, or her father, who wasn't here, for support. She had learned everything she knew alone. Yes, she had made some new friends on her travels, and they had proven time and again that they cared for her and promised to protect her. But could she put her life in the giant's hands? Could she face her fears and trust what he had told her about his dreams? And hers? She wasn't sure she was ready for such a huge commitment.

She looked at her enormous friend and her tiny friend who hovered nearby. The giant's eyes were full of love for her, and the pixie looked like she wanted to fly straight into battle with her.

Charlie sat on the dry, brown grass and opened her pack. She reached into the bottom and pulled out the letter her father had hidden there. She read through it again and reflected on his words.

I have enclosed a vial of the Deep Spring water. Keep it safe, as it will be a valuable asset to you on your journey. The giant should have explained the significance of the water by now.

The Deep Spring water had already been a valuable asset for her. It had helped her get close to Jessamine and find the map. Of course, she hadn't done anything. Pepper and the giant were responsible for finding the map and getting Charlie out safely.

This also made Pepper's idea about drinking the water at just the right moment seem like a better one. It had already been valuable, but now it might come in useful, too. It may save her life.

I know what you are capable of and I know you have a good heart. Keep your friends close and pay attention to all of your dreams while you travel. They will tell you the things you should do.

Charlie was glad for this advice. If she hadn't kept her friends close and paid attention to her dreams, she wouldn't have survived all the things she had already been through. They had all done so much for her already. And she had hardly done anything for them. She probably still had a part to play in all of this. Otherwise, her dreams wouldn't still be leading her here.

What you, the giant, and others you will meet on the way, are about to accomplish is bigger than me, or you, or our home. It is for the future of the entire world. You have been chosen for a reason. Make good choices and you will do great things; more than you think you are capable of.

Charlie's eyes filled with tears. Her father had been right about everything else. She had already survived more in the past few weeks than she ever had to face in all the years before. She let the words sink in: What you are about to accomplish is for the future of the entire world. Was she ready to let the fate of the world rest on her shoulders? Could she put her trust in her friends once and for all and accept whatever the outcome would be?

She decided that if she was honest with herself, she wasn't sure she would be able to awaken the giants and save everyone. But she knew, deep down inside, because of the words of her father and friends, that she had to try.

She wiped her eyes and folded the note from her father back up and placed it back at the bottom of her bag. She would do it. She would climb into the ball and do her best to awaken the giants before it was too late.

But before she could speak, Pepper called from her lookout above. Eyes wide with panic, she hollered, "There are more of Jessamine's beasts coming. They are gaining, fast!"

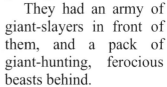

They had an army of giant-slayers in front of them, and a pack of giant-hunting, ferocious beasts behind.

"Help me into the ball!" she called to the giant. "I'm ready!"

He opened it and she climbed in. He picked up the open ball and brought it close to his face. He looked into her eyes and spoke with a firm voice. "Charlie, you will be safe."

She waited as he swallowed several times and blinked away tears. "I love you."

Before Charlie had a chance to respond he snapped the ball shut. Charlie was alone in the darkness.

Charlie knew that the giant, in his own way, had been saying good-bye to her, and there was nothing she could do to stop the chain of events that had been set into motion. All she could do now was wait.

She took the stopper out of the vial and filled her mouth with the sweet, cool water from home. It was hard not to swallow it; it tasted so much better than the water she had been drinking for weeks now. She held it in her mouth to wait for the right time when she would need it to save her life.

Chapter 32

Charlie knew what happened on the outside, based on the plans they had made. And from the way the giant moved, and the sounds that were all around her. The giant held the ball against his chest with one hand and drew his sword with the other. He ran with all his might toward the army that stretched as far as they could see. The beasts would be closing in behind him.

She held on tight to the straps that dangled from the ceiling of the ball as she jostled around. The darkness was penetrating, and she tried to focus on not swallowing the water in her mouth.

The giant let out a mighty battle cry as he drew nearer to the human army. She could hear the terrified and angry response from the men on the ground. She felt his cadence change when he swept the men aside with his sword. He blazed a path through the soldiers towards the ravine. She could hear the ranks close behind him as he pushed his way through, but she could tell he did not slow. Not yet anyway.

She held the water in her mouth with all of her willpower and braced herself against one curved side of the ball.

Later she would discover that Pepper had darted in and out of the army, biting and burning as many of the giant-slayers as she could to distract them from the giant.

Charlie could also hear the beasts attack, and the frantic cries of the men as the beasts attacked the men as readily as they attacked the giant. It gave the giant the advantage he needed to make it all the way through the mass of men and weapons.

Inside the ball, Charlie jolted and bumped around. She could feel the vibrations of every hit the giant took and felt his gait slow. He was being attacked but she had no idea how much damage was being done to him or their enemy. She wished she could do something to help, but all she could do was stand in the dark.

As her fear threatened to overwhelm her, she focused on her breathing. She checked and rechecked the sword in her right hand, the sling shoved in her belt and the bag of round rocks that dangled next to it. She had the Key of Sariah in reach in the pack strapped to her back alongside her supply of arrows and bow.

Charlie envisioned in her mind what she needed to do. She knew she would be able to feel herself fly through the air, and how to tell when she began the descent. Once she felt that falling sensation, she would deploy the parachute and prepare to spring out of the ball. She would swallow the water and face any men on the ground.

She would not fail. She couldn't. All she had to do was get the Key of Sariah to the right place in time. The giant would be out of danger. She would have to be fast on her feet and swift to take out the soldiers that she knew she would encounter on the way.

Charlie could tell the moment the giant shot the ball across the gorge. She could hear the cries of the men as they overtook the giant. Her stomach dropped to the floor. The sensation was nauseating, and the knowledge of what her friends now faced without her didn't help.

She knew the giant would be doing his best to fend off the army and beasts, while Pepper would burn her way through them and pierce them like a winged molten arrow.

The ball that held Charlie made a smooth arc in the sky over the ravine. Charlie's mind raced. The trajectory of the ball reached its peak. She began to descend.

She hit the parachute release lever. She expected to be jolted as the chute opened and pulled the ball from its freefall. But the ball continued to fall with increasing speed. Charlie slammed the lever over and over with her fist, willing the parachute to open. She continued to fall. There was no way she would survive the impact.

At the precise moment she had this thought, the ball slammed into the earth on the other side of the ravine. It knocked the wind out of Charlie. Before she could think of swallowing, she hit her head on the side of the ball. Everything went instantly dark.

Chapter 33

The ball split open and a beam of light shone a stripe on Charlie's face. She winced as she came to and tried to register her surroundings. The first thing she became aware of was that she wasn't dead. This fact surprised her. The jolt of landing must have forced the water down her throat. The water had saved her when she should not have survived. She didn't want to move in case the healing hadn't finished, and she had some terrible injury.

She quickly and methodically tested each part of her body for injury or pain. She heard voices outside. She stilled. She took short breaths and tried to focus so she could figure out what the soldiers were saying.

The men were trying to decide if the girl inside the ball was alive or dead, and, if she was alive, what they should do with her. She listened as they assumed she was with the giant that the rest of the army battled across the gorge. They weren't sure if they should just kill her, too. They came to the conclusion to jab her with a sword to see if she was alive.

Charlie didn't hesitate. She burst from the ball. She slashed her sword through the air. She took down the nearest soldier. Before the other soldiers had time to react, she pierced one in the chest and knocked another down with a sweep-kick. As she pulled her sword out of a fallen body, the other two soldiers closed in. The movements came without thought, just like the giant had said. She defended the attacks and managed to bash one of the soldiers in the head, knocking him out. She sent the last soldier flying backwards as his sword fell from his hands.

She stood and panted in the middle of the carnage. She looked at each man in turn. She was very lucky that she had the element of surprise and the potency of the water on her side. The effects of the water on her body were intense. Her strength and reflexes were heightened. She recovered so quickly from each attack that the wounds she received had no effect on her.

She felt a rush of renewed energy and checked her weapons. She jogged up the mountainside. As she climbed higher, she made her way to the front of the mountain. She couldn't see the ravine on the other side where she knew the giant faced a formidable fight. If she woke the other giants in time, they would come and help her giant before it was too late. She knew they didn't have much time. She needed to hurry.

Hot from her climb up the mountain, Charlie stumbled over the mass of boulders. She saw the Valley of Giants below her, though it would be hidden from any other angle, and she could tell that it could be missed by anyone who may wander the mountains if they didn't know it was there.

The valley started right up against the mountainside and stretched outward toward the plains. It ended in a high cliff above the ravine. The whole thing did resemble the shape of a horn.

Near the center of the valley stood a pedestal with a weathered metal tube connected to either side of it. The tube stretched from the pedestal to the back of the valley, anchored to the side of the mountain, and the height of the peak. On the other end of the pedestal, the tube ran the length of the valley and flared out right at the edge of the cliff. On the pedestal itself was a gap in the tube. Charlie could easily see that the Key of Sariah she had in her pack would be a perfect fit.

Christine Marshall

Chapter 34

Charlie scanned the edge of the valley and prepared to slide down the side from where she stood. Before she started, a band of soldiers entered the valley from the other side, nearest the cliff. She knew she didn't have much time to reach the pedestal before they saw her. If they noticed her before she placed the Key, she would fail.

She ducked behind a boulder to gather her thoughts and prepare herself for another fight. She reached in her bag and took out the Key of Sariah, tied a length of thin cord around it and hung it around her neck. She tore a couple of finger-sized pieces off the hem of her tunic, wadded them, and stuffed them in her ears to help dull the sound of the Battle Horn once she activated it. She touched the sling on her waist to make sure it was ready and opened the bag of stones wide for easy access. Her sword was secured on her other side and her dagger was in the strap around her ankle. She took her bow from its sheath, loaded it with an arrow, and fingered the last three on her back. She took a deep breath and crept out from behind the boulder.

The soldiers did not advance very fast through the valley. They milled around near the cliff and watched the battle below. Charlie picked her way down the hillside near the back of the valley.

She was dying to go faster. She had anticipated running down, slamming the Key in place, waking the giants, and her friends would be saved. Now, instead of speeding down the hill, she moved at a snail's pace. She was anxious to make it to the bottom but didn't want to blow it and have to waste more time fighting, or worse, lose her chance to engage the Key at all.

When she was about halfway down, she slipped. A few pebbles tumbled down the hillside. The soldiers looked up. They shouted to one another when they spotted her.

She sprang into action. She'd never missed a target before. This would be just like hitting her targets back home. No problem.

She stood and unleashed the arrow ready in her bow. It zipped through the air and pierced the armor of the foremost soldier, dropping him to the ground. The other soldiers cried out and raced toward her. She let the other three arrows fly, one right after the other, dropping three more of the soldiers in their paths. Ten more headed her way.

She took a deep breath and sprinted down the hill. She tossed the bow to the ground with one hand and pulled the sling from her belt with the other. She loaded it with three smooth stones and paused to let off a shot. She continued her race toward the pedestal. Her shot hit the face of another soldier. He cried out in agony as he dropped to his knees. She let out three more shots before she reached the bottom, stopping three more soldiers in their tracks. Three soldiers were ahead of the rest as they made their way toward her. She leapt the last distance off the hillside, crouched into her landing, then shot forward with all the speed she could muster. The Deep Spring water did its job. She ran faster and harder than she ever had before.

She yanked the Key of Sariah, which snapped the cord at the back of her neck. She unsheathed her sword with her other hand. She jumped onto a large rock near the pedestal and made a leap through the air. She landed hard on the pedestal. Charlie jammed the Key of Sariah in place.

The earth trembled. The soldiers closed in on her. She jumped and crouched, breath coming fast, her back to the pedestal. She waited for something to happen.

The first soldier rounded the corner. He managed to slash her leg with his sword before she jumped at him. She slashed his arm with her own sword. The pain in her leg was intense, but quickly dissipated as the Deep Spring water worked its magic. Two more soldiers rounded the corner, swords at the ready. She waited for the opportune moment to strike as they prowled around her.

All at once the ground violently shook and a loud noise blasted out the end of the valley. It reverberated across the plains. Charlie and the last of the soldiers stumbled.

The soldiers positioned themselves on either side of Charlie. Both men used their swords to slash and stab at her. She managed to dodge most of their advances, their aim not being true due to the shaking earth. And the ear-shattering noise.

She ignored the pain of the few hits, feinted to one side, then pushed her sword into the side of the soldier on the right. As he fell to the ground she faced off with the final attacker. Her breaths were hard and fast. She needed to take him down.

He was distracted. The noise that had emerged from the Horn bounced back and forth along the walls of the narrow valley. The soldiers still at the end of the valley had dropped to the ground, hands over their ears. Charlie used this momentary distraction to wound the leg of the soldier before her so he could not stand.

She stumbled away from the pedestal and headed toward the back of the valley. She couldn't see the battle below from where she stood, so she climbed the hillside to a ledge in order to obtain a better vantage point. She could now see everything happening across the ravine.

Her wounds knit themselves back together. But her heart did not slow. She spotted the giant right away, surrounded by swarms of men. She could tell he was wounded; his head was bleeding from the back. Her heart seized in her chest.

She had to do something. Anything. But what?

The tremendous sound from the Horn echoed through the valley. Just as the shock wave of sound reached the edge of the battle, Charlie screamed. The giant was struck in the back by a huge boulder. It knocked him down. He continued to struggle. As soon as he hit the ground, the men clambered on top of him. They shot him with their giant-slaying cross bows. They pierced the armor and the arrow sunk deep into

his chest. At the same moment, the sound of the horn swept through the army.

The men were immediately knocked down from the noise. They clutched their heads and curled into balls at the sound. Charlie stood frozen to the ledge. Tears streamed down her cheeks. Each breath came as a gasp.

The giant bled form his many wounds. He struggled for breath. The ground shook around him. He shifted slightly toward her and swept the men from his body with one weak arm. He turned his head so that his eyes met Charlie's from so far away.

Impossibly, through all the tumult of the screaming men and the thunder of the Battle Horn, she heard him whisper right into her ear, "I'm sorry." She could only watch as his chest fell and he closed his eyes for the last time.

At that moment every other sound in the entire world was silenced for Charlie. She collapsed onto the ledge and sobbed. She had accomplished her goal. Giants began to awaken around the edge of the prairie, in the mountains, and beyond; but she had also failed her friend. She hadn't been fast enough. Her friend was gone.

Christine Marshall

Chapter 35

The noise of the Battle Horn radiated throughout the land. It grew in volume as it traveled, rather than dissipate. It reached the giants who slumbered far and wide. It awakened many giants close enough to the battle to be of immediate assistance.

What appeared to be grassy hills of earth in the prairie, rocky outcroppings on hillsides, and mossy boulders in forests, turned out to be giants camouflaged by hundreds of years of sleep in their natural surroundings. These inanimate parts of the earth moved as soon as the sound of the Battle Horn reached them.

The giants, one by one, blinked their eyes open, broke their arms free of the nature that enveloped them, wiped earth and plant life from their faces and bodies, and, with stiff movements, hoisted themselves from the ground. They each in turn faced the direction of the Battle Horn, and the sound of thousands of soldiers crying out in rage or pain. One by one, they ran toward the battle.

Charlie watched through puffy eyes as more and more giants emerged. They attacked the men doubled over from the sound of the horn. They lobbed huge glacier rocks at the army and flattened dozens of men at a time. They grabbed the catapults the men had built, and heaved them onto the soldiers on the ground, like they were toys. They swung their massive fists, leveling hundreds of men with each swing. They made their way to their fallen friend and fought to defend his body, as well as to defeat the army. They killed thousands of soldiers between them, while thousands more fled, deserting their army in exchange for survival.

The men who stayed regained their footing and fought the giants. They managed to overtake two of them and kill one with the giant-slaying weapons before they were killed by other giants. The other was injured and could no longer stand or fight.

Pepper winged her way across the ravine and up the mountainside in search of Charlie. She found Charlie folded in on herself. Blood soaked through her tattered clothes. Pepper alighted on Charlie's arm, patted her back, and sang quiet pixie songs of comfort to her heartbroken friend. She shed warm tears, which dripped onto Charlie's skin and magically soothed Charlie until she was able to slow her breathing and open her eyes.

"Thank you," Charlie whispered as more silent tears rolled down her cheeks.

The two friends picked themselves up and headed toward the ravine to see what the outcome of the battle would be. On their way through the small valley, Charlie removed the Key of Sariah from the Battle Horn. The Horn was silenced.

The intense noise from the Horn had toppled pillars of rock and formed a makeshift bridge across the ravine. Charlie made her way across. Pepper flew so close to Charlie that she could feel the heat from the anger that still lit the pixie's hair.

Charlie needed to get to the giant. She needed to be with him. Her wounds had healed, but she was exhausted from battle and grief. She swung her sword to fend off attacks from the men but was soon outnumbered.

Pepper motioned at one of the giants. He took two long steps, flattening many soldiers into the ground, and reached down to scoop Charlie onto his shoulder. Without missing a beat, he resumed his fight.

Charlie watched Pepper fight alongside the giants. She zipped around, dropping human solders like flies. The battle lasted for what seemed like forever. The strongest of the warriors refused to give up. Eventually, the giant slayers were defeated. There were no survivors of the army on the battlefield. The only survivors were the ones who had fled.

Chapter 36

The giants watched the last of the stragglers run towards the horizon. They gathered at the body of Charlie's friend. Charlie was lowered to stand on his chest. She stared at his still face. Tears ran in steady streams down her cheeks. Pepper stayed close. Charlie could feel the breeze from her fast-beating wings. Charlie knelt and placed a hand on the giant. She closed her eyes and spoke to the giant in her head. Silently, she thanked him for his sacrifice, and apologized to him for not sounding the Horn in time.

Charlie let her hand fall to her side. She opened her eyes. It was so quiet around her. There had been so much noise during the battle, and it had lasted for so long, that the silence was almost painful. She turned around to see where the other giants had gone. Her eyes widened at the sight before her.

All around Charlie and her giant, a hundred other giants stood, eyes on Charlie. She hadn't noticed how many there were before. She was so caught up in the battle and the painful aftermath. Each oversized man was as solid and strong as the next. Most were impossibly taller than her own friend. Some panted heavily from the battle, others nursed wounds. All paid respects to their fallen comrades.

Thousands of dead human soldiers littered the ground in a huge circle around the giants. The prairie was stained with blood. Patches of ground burned from Pepper's fire. Scattered here and there were the remains of various catapult and giant-slaying contraptions that had been torn to shreds by the giants. Swords, spears, bows and arrows, and shields were strewn about. Charlie's stomach lurched.

After several minutes, Charlie spoke to the nearest giant. "Thank you for saving me, and for fighting."

"You are very welcome. You and your friends have sacrificed a great deal on our behalf. We are honored to serve you." He closed his eyes and bowed his head as he finished his sentence. He stretched out his hand. "Please, come."

Charlie stared at the dirty, bloody hand before her. "Go... where?" she asked.

"To the City of Giants."

"Yes, of course." She turned her gaze to her friend, then stepped onto the outstretched hand.

The giants worked together to carry the bodies of their fallen back to their city. As they journeyed, they were joined by other awakened giants who gathered to their home. The mood was somber. The giants spoke only as necessary. Charlie rode on the shoulder of the one she had spoken with earlier. Pepper continued to float by her side.

Chapter 37

The funeral for the giants took place in a great gathering hall in the heart of the City of Giants. It was quiet. The bodies rested on elevated slabs. Each person could approach, one by one, to pay their respects. When it was Charlie's turn, all of the giants in attendance turned to face her. They formed an aisle for her to pass through.

Charlie heard a strange thumping noise as she walked toward the front of the hall. It took her a moment to figure out that it was the sound of all the giants hearts beating. The sound felt symbolic of the kindness and gentleness of all the giants that surrounded her now.

She made her way toward her friend where she was met again by the same giant she had come to know on their way home. He looked at her with a sad smile and lifted her to stand once more near her friend's still body. He stepped away.

Charlie knelt and rested her head on her friend's chest. There, she let the tears flow once again.

"Why?" she whispered. "You said you would be safe." She choked on her words. "You promised that we would both be safe. How could you do this? How could you leave me?"

Charlie's shoulders shook with her sobs. This was all too much.

Her mind was quiet. She cried. Then, out of the blue, Charlie heard the giant's voice, inside her own mind. "I did what I had to do."

She froze. Was it her imagination? How could it be anything else?

"But you said you would be safe... you promised," she whispered.

"Charlie," his voice was real. She dared not open her eyes, in case it would stop. "I am sorry. It was the only way for you to be able to do what needed to be done. If you had known, you wouldn't have gone through with it. I didn't say I would be safe, I said I would be fine. And I am." His voice was so calm. Peace engulfed Charlie.

He was right. If she had known, she wouldn't have gone through with it.

"But how are you fine?" None of this made any sense.

"I knew long before I ever met you how I would meet the end of my life. As we embarked on our journey together, the dreams stayed the same. I was not afraid to die, Charlie, for I knew that my death would mean that you, and so many others, would live."

"It's not fair," Charlie whispered as tears slipped down her cheeks. "You shouldn't have had to die. Not for me, not for anyone! If we had gone faster, or I had tried harder, or fought better, none of this would have happened. I would have reached the Battle Horn in time and you would have lived. I failed you..." her sobs returned.

"No. This is how it was meant to be. It always has been, and nothing you could have done would have changed it. Sometimes we must experience hard things, but they help us become better versions of ourselves."

That was what Gerfott had told her. And her father.

"You would not have become the woman you need to become if it wasn't for this experience. These things you have done- the sacrifices you have made- they will all help you to face greater trials in your future. You will accomplish much, Little Dreamer."

She didn't know what to think. She knew he spoke the truth, but she didn't want to hear it. It was all too raw still.

"Do you remember what I said to you just before I shut the ball?" the giant asked.

"Yes," Charlie recalled his hasty good-bye and I love you.

"It will always be true. I will always love you. And as you go throughout your life, you will feel that love and it will help sustain you in difficult times. Never forget the love from your family and friends."

The words warmed her heart as his voice faded. He was gone, really gone, now. She cried for some time longer before she sat up and signaled for the attending giant to help her to the floor.

She stood outside, eyes closed. She let her tears dry. She allowed the sun to warm her. Just like the love of her father, and the giant.

Before she opened her eyes, she heard a musical sound reach into her heart. She looked around. Where did it come from? Something in the sky caught her eye. A large, bright red and orange bird. It was the phoenix! It had regrown. It was amazing! Its tail feathers were as long as Charlie was tall, soft and feathery, and a brilliant crimson. Its wings were defined, with various shades of red and orange, and they looked like a flame when outstretched. The plume on its head waved in the wind. It reminded Charlie of Pepper's hair when it was aflame. The sound of its song calmed her mind and lifted her troubled heart. Juliette sat gracefully on the bird's back, both legs to one side.

Several other oversized birds and butterflies carried others of Juliette's people and followed close behind.

Charlie smiled to herself. Juliette sure knew how to make an entrance.

Juliette hugged Charlie tight, and Charlie's tears leaked out once more.

The Princess stepped back, though her hands stayed on Charlie's shoulders. "Thank you, Charlie." She looked deep into Charlie's eyes.

Charlie shook her head. "I should be thanking you! You have done so much for me, for us. We couldn't have done this without your help and the help of your people. You have no idea how grateful I am."

Juliette shook her head. "You have sacrificed far more for all living things than anyone could ever realize. You deserve to be remembered by all."

Charlie blushed. She gave Juliette a small nod.

The two embraced one more time before Juliette led her group into the great hall to see their fallen friend. As the group passed, each of Juliette's people nodded to Charlie, or grasped her hand, squeezed her arm, or hugged her close, and whispered their thanks one-by-one.

That night, much to Charlie's surprise, she dreamed of home.

Chapter 38

The following morning Charlie entered the banquet hall. She stopped in the entrance, struck by the number of people gathered together. They ate and talked in small clumps. Some laughed at the good memories of those they had lost. Others cried at hopes unfulfilled.

Charlie joined Juliette at her table where her people were gathered around her. As she sat, something pricked her neck.

"Pepper!" Charlie cried. "I'm sorry I have been so distracted the past few days."

"It's fine, I understand! How are you feeling?" the pixie inquired.

"A little better. My heart still hurts, but I think I'll be fine." Her voice was steady for the first time since the battle. "How about you?"

"I don't think I'll ever let you out of my sight again!" Pepper kissed Charlie's cheek with her hot little kisses. Charlie giggled.

Charlie spent the day with Pepper and Juliette. She told Juliette everything she had seen and done since the last time they had met. She asked the Princess about the battle the dragons fought, since she had missed the outcome.

"Many dragons were lost," Juliette told her. "Nearly half that fought that day."

Charlie stayed quiet. It was all so unfair.

"They knew what they were fighting for," Juliette continued. "The giant-slayers army has been defeated, the dark creatures have been destroyed, and the giants have been awakened. The Deep Spring will be protected now, and these evil people will die one day, just as they should. They will not be able to harness the immortality of the Deep Spring, and the threat of them unleashing their evil on all the good in the world has come to an end.

"Many dragons died," Juliette continued. "Our friend is gone. There has been much loss in this battle. But it is over now. We have won." Juliette squeezed Charlie's arm reassuringly.

"But what about Jessamine? Won't she be furious that her army was defeated and her pack of beasts destroyed?" Fear pricked the back of her mind.

"I did not realize you had not heard! Jessamine is in prison. It seems that her creation of the dark creatures and her control over the army was unsanctioned by the city leaders. They had been searching for her for some time in order to imprison her and halt her control. She eluded them again and again. When the giant broke open her home, it roused suspicions. They all thought Jessamine was long gone, along with her influence over the army. Her whereabouts were uncovered by our friend when he rescued you. She is no longer a threat to you or anyone else."

"Are you sure? Doesn't she have connections, and alliances?" Charlie wanted to believe it to be true.

Juliette squeezed her hand. "You have nothing left to worry about. Trust me!"

Charlie nodded. But she recalled the words from her friend, about being prepared for future troubles. If this was all over, then there wouldn't be future troubles that she would need to be prepared for, would there? She put the idea out of her mind for now and wandered around. She talked to people and giants she had not met. She told her story over and over until she felt like she never wanted to talk again.

She came upon the giant who helped her back to the city.

The giant squatted and looked intently at Charlie. "What will you do know, young friend?" he asked her.

"I'm not sure…"

"I know what your friend told you at the burial ceremony," he stated.

"What? How?" Shock washed over her.

"Come, Charlie. Let us walk." He rested his hand to the ground and invited her to climb on.

She relaxed on his shoulder. After they had moved away from the milling crowd, Charlie expected the giant to begin. She waited what felt like forever. Was he waiting for her to ask?

She needed to know. She asked him to tell her.

"We have the ability to share our dreams. He shared this one with me. He also asked me to help you."

Of course, her friend would want someone like himself to look after Charlie. But she didn't think she could handle growing close to another friend, only to end up losing someone else. Her heart felt guarded.

She waited for him to continue.

"There is much for you to accomplish in your life. You will have many more great adventures."

Did she want more adventures like this one?

"But it is time for you to return home." The giant finished.

Her long years behind the wall seemed like a distant memory, but she could see her home and father in her mind as clear as if they were before her now. She had seen and done so much in the months she had been gone. She didn't want to go on another adventure, but she wasn't sure she wanted to go home yet, either. Back to a life where everything remained the same year after year. She felt torn inside at the desire to see her father mingled with the urge to continue to see the world. In the end, she wanted rest and quiet.

"I will take you home. We will leave tomorrow." The giant interrupted Charlie's thoughts.

She turned to look at his face. He stood on the hill above the city, and they could see it stretched out before them. It bustled with activity. Charlie couldn't believe how deserted it had been the first time she had come here.

But nothing was the same. It didn't matter where she went or what she tried to do next, everything was different. She was different. She had taken lives and saved lives. She had learned to trust others and had opened her heart to friendship and love. She had made a new enemy, but so many more new friends.

"I knew your mother, Charlie." The giant interrupted her thoughts again. His confession startled her. "She was a great friend of mine. You are becoming a great woman, just as she was. She wasn't ready to return home when her time came, either. She learned the hard way. Now, it is time for you to return home."

Charlie felt like her heart would beat out of her chest. She had never known anyone that remembered her mother besides her own father. She had so many questions she wanted to ask but wasn't sure she wanted to hear the whole story yet, either. She submitted to what the giant had said, about taking her home.

"I understand. I will be ready."

He nodded. "That is good."

Chapter 39

Charlie bid farewell to Juliette and the other forest people. She said goodbye to the few giants she had met and talked to and rubbed a few animals behind the ears.

She picked up her pack. Pepper hovered nearby.

"I am going home," she told the pixie.

"I know, you told me," Pepper stated.

How was she supposed to say goodbye to Pepper? She tried to think of something to say.

"Where will you go next?" she finally asked in an attempt to fill the awkward silence.

Pepper's hair and skin began to glow. "What do you mean?"

"I mean, will you find other pixies to live with?"

Pepper's hair lit up. "No! I thought I was going with you!" Her face looked angry.

Charlie's eyebrows shot up. Her eyes misted with tears. "Really?"

"What?" Pepper snapped. "After everything we've been through you think I would just let you leave?" Her arms were folded tightly across her chest.

Charlie took a step toward the pixie. "Of course, I want you to come with me! I just didn't know what to expect, I guess."

"Great!" Her hair and skin instantly returned to normal.

"Were you getting angry with me?" Charlie asked, a sly grin on her face.

"I thought you didn't want me to come, that's all. There's no way I'm leaving you now. Besides, it's in my nature to want to protect you. How could I live with myself if I just let you leave and never knew what happened to you?"

Charlie laughed. "I love you too, Pepper!"

Pepper stayed near Charlie, closer than usual, after that.

Charlie took one last long look at everyone, then turned to step on the giant's hand.

"Charlie, wait!" she heard from the crowd.

She watched as Alder emerged from the people gathered around her.

He stopped close enough that his presence calmed her. He pulled something out of his pocket and held it out in his palms.

"A gift, to remember me by," he gazed at her with his deep brown eyes.

Nestled in his hands was a beautiful flower. The blossom was a pale turquoise blue with fine white veins throughout each of the five petals, and a thin green stem with long leaves.

"What is it?" Charlie asked. She couldn't take her eyes off the unusual blossom.

"An ever-blooming heart lily. It's really rare. It looks fragile, but it's actually quite resilient. If kept near light, the blossom will never close."

Pepper oohed and aaahed over the blossom and wondered out loud if the nectar was tasty.

Alder chuckled at Pepper, then spoke to Charlie once more. He met her eyes and spoke in a smooth, quiet voice. "I hope when you see it you will think about yourself." He rested his palms in her outstretched hands. He slid his hands from beneath the blossom and cradled her hands in his as she held the blossom. His strong, dark hands made hers look small and pale in comparison. "You may feel insignificant at times, but your worth is more than you can imagine."

Charlie was a little breathless. Her hands tingled where Alder held them. She kept her eyes glued to his as he continued.

"You can do anything you decide to do. You are resilient, and strong, just like this flower. And you are beautiful too." He beamed as he leaned in close and kissed her lightly on the cheek. Charlie blushed and pulled the blossom closer to her heart.

"Thank you," she managed to say as her eyes watered. "I will never forget you."

"Nor I you, Charlie. I will find you again, I promise. In the meantime, I believe you should begin your journey home. I am sure you are missed." He stepped away. She couldn't take her eyes off him.

Pepper pinched her on the neck, and Charlie started. "Oh, right. Well, I guess this is it…"

She hesitated for a second before she climbed onto the giant's hand. He lifted her to his shoulder and turned away from his home to carry her toward hers.

She waved over her shoulder at the crowd gathered to watch her depart. One last tear slid down her cheek at the thought of all of the love she had found out here.

Charlie felt comfortable riding on a giant's shoulder for her journey home, while two more giants accompanied them. Charlie had no idea how far away they were or how long it would take to get there. She passed the time by talking to Pepper about life within the wall, and asked the giants questions about their own personal histories. These giants were much older than her fallen friend. The one whose shoulder she rested was the same one who carried her away from the battle. She learned he was almost five thousand years old. He had been present for the ogre wars that had unified the giants. And he remembered the battle that the giants and humans fought alongside one another. The others were old, too, but not as old as he was. She was young compared to them! They each had rich, long histories full of adventure, love, and lots of sleeping.

The most surprising thing she learned was the giant's name. "Tearlach, but please, call me Charles."

She asked Charles about her mother at last. He told her about how determined and brave she had been. About her stubborn streak, which made Charlie smile to herself, for she was also stubborn. He told of the great love she had had for Charlie's father, which made Charlie's heart sing. It was so good to hear someone say such kind things about her mother.

"I once accompanied your mother home following a great battle, as well, Charlie. She had loved the adventurous life she had found, and was reluctant to return. She delayed her return for quite some time, in fact. But soon she realized she was expecting you, and knew it was past the time to return. I began calling the baby within her 'Little Charlie' as I carried her home."

So that's where the name Charlie had come from! Her father had either not known, or had decided not to remember.

Charles continued. "She died shortly after you were born, as you know, but before she made it home. Sariah was a dear friend, and I have never stopped missing her."

"Wait, did you call her 'Sariah'?" Charlie asked in a hurry.

"Yes, that is the name she seemed to prefer."

"My father always called her Sara…"

"I believe that he was the only one who knew her by that name. Something special between the two," the giant explained.

"And she fought in a great battle, alongside the giants?" Charlie asked. The pieces started to fit together at last.

"Yes, she was pivotal in the giant's involvement. Why do you ask these questions Charlie? Is there something you wish to know?"

Charlie swallowed. Her heart rate increased, and her stomach felt funny. "Is she…" the question burned in her mind, but putting it into words was difficult. "Is she the same Sariah… that the Key of Sariah was named after?"

"Yes, of course she is, Charlie. Did you not know? She was a hero." Charles said matter-of-factly.

Charlie's head spun. She knew she looked like her mother; she had learned she had some of the same personality traits and characteristics as her mother, but she never would have guessed that she had followed directly in her mother's footsteps.

It took the giants a week to carry Charlie home. Still, she wasn't prepared for the flood of emotions that overwhelmed her when she saw the wall. It had the same construction style as the City of Giants.

The homesickness she had suppressed for months overcame her and she let out a cry. Tears escaped from her eyes. She was ready to go home.

They arrived at a different place than where Charlie had ridden the waterfall out. The giants walked right to a secluded, vine-covered area along the base of the wall. They poked around a bit, then showed Charlie a secret entrance that opened to a hollow space within the wall. There was a ladder to climb, with light that shone down the shaft from above. They told her that the ladder led to another hidden point on the other side, high above her head.

The three giants knelt before Charlie. They placed their fists over their hearts. They bowed before her and pledged their allegiance. Charles explained to Charlie that she could contact them through her dreams, just as her friend had done before. Then they bid her farewell.

"Good-bye, my little Charlie," Charles whispered as he turned away.

Christine Marshall

Chapter 40

Charlie walked through the village while Pepper hovered nearby. She was struck at how much nothing had changed here. The people, the rhythm, the way of life, was the same as always. Folks entered and left shops as they bought things they needed. They met on the dirt road to visit and catch up with one another. There was no hurry to anything. They had no idea how close they had come to destruction and extinction.

Charlie made her way down the path that led to her home. She needed to gather her courage to see her father. She swallowed to stifle the tears that wanted to come.

She saw her father move around inside her home. She took a deep breath and opened the door. She called out to him in a small voice as she entered.

Her father dropped the dish he had been washing and it clattered to the floor. He rushed to Charlie. He swallowed her in his arms before she had time to close the door behind her. She basked in the warmth of his embrace, and stood there for a very long time as she squeezed him back as tight as she could.

Pepper floated about them and waited for them to finish hugging. Charlie's father released her just enough to look into her eyes. He cradled her face in both of his large, rough hands.

"Charlie! Oh, Charlie!" He held her close again.

The two held each other for several more minutes before her father was ready to let her go. She finished entering the house and set her pack down.

She motioned at Pepper with one hand and wiped the tears from her cheeks with the other. "Dad, this is Pepper."

Pepper swooped and gave him a mischievous pinch on the arm, then zoomed around him a few times. Charlie grinned. "She's a pixie."

Her father chuckled, but never took his eyes off of Charlie. "I've missed you."

"Me too, Dad.

Charlie settled into her chair by the fire and began the long process of telling her father everything from the beginning. She asked him questions about her mother. She learned that her mother had been a Dreamer, too. She wanted to know all about the battle her mother had been instrumental in winning and was shocked to find out that Jessamine had been a major player in that battle as well. Charlie's mother had been pregnant with Charlie when she had left to find Jessamine but hadn't known yet. Within a few months of meeting Charles, it became evident that she was expecting. She continued her mission, however, and fought in the battle that Charles had told her about. Having received a serious wound from a magical weapon that would not heal, Sariah had known that her time in this world was coming to an end. Charles had told Charlie's father that Sariah had been heartbroken at the thought of never meeting Charlie, and never seeing the love of her life again. Her grief was complete as she passed during childbirth.

Charlie and her dad both ended up in tears remembering her mother. They talked long into the night, and Charlie headed to bed just before dawn.

In the early predawn hours when everything is cool and damp, Charlie snuggled deep under her covers. She felt truly at peace for the first time in ages. But as she drifted into sleep, images flashed through her mind.

A withered, weak-looking Jessamine whispered through the bars of her dungeon cell to a dark, hooded figure.

Jessamine, who looked younger and stronger, though still in her prison.

The wall of one side of Jessamine's cell burst outward, and the whole dungeon shook and crumbled.

A huge, dirty hand reached into Jessamine's cell and lifted her out.

Other giants, all dressed in black dragon leather, destroyed the prison.

The giant who carried Jessamine on his shoulder strode away, and Jessamine looked back and stared right at Charlie. A triumphant smirk spread across her face.

Charlie's eyes flew open. She jumped out of bed, called to Pepper, and rushed down the hall to where her dad read by the fire.

"Dad!" she cried as Pepper flew around and turned red from all the excitement. "I've had another dream!" Charlie exclaimed.

"I know, Charlie." He closed the book in his hand and stood to face her. "I have, too."

THE END

Read more of Charlie's story!
in the *Charlie and the Giants* series.

Available on Amazon and CMarshallFantasy Etsy shop

Christine's ***Charlie and the Giants*** books are filled with magic, mythical creatures, and an *awesome* female protagonist that has to figure out who she wants to become.

If you love books that will help you forget the real world for a little while, are full of surprising characters, and will keep you guessing, then these are the perfect books for you!

Read Jessamine's, Juliette's, and Sariah's origin stories in *A Series of Retellings*

Jessamine   Juliette   Sariah

The first three books in the *Charlie and the Giants* series. Learn why Jessamine became so wicked. Find out why Juliette loves the giants so much. Read Sariah's inspiring but heartbreaking story. These origin stories for three of the critical characters in the *Charlie and the Giants* series are framed as fairytale retellings full of twists and turns that you'll never see coming.

Available on Amazon and CMarshallFantasy Etsy shop

Thanks for Reading!

I hope you enjoyed this book!
Please leave a review on Amazon and Goodreads. For indie authors like me, reviews are our lifeblood. Help a girl out, it'll only take a few minutes!

Check me out on social media!

TikTok: www.tiktok.com/@christinemarshallfantasy

Amazon: the_christine_marshall
https://www.amazon.com/author/the_christine_marshall

CMarshallFantasy on Etsy- for signed copies and free swag!

Facebook: Christine K. Marshall-author
www.facebook.com/christinemarshallauthor

Instagram: @the_christine_marshall_24
www.instagram.com/the_christine_marshall_24

Goodreads: Christine_Marshall
    www.goodreads.com/author/show/22364476.Christine Marshall

Email: christinemarshall24@gmail.com

Acknowledgments

To my beta readers **Sumedha, Cynthia, Belle, Sophie**, and **Pepper**, thank you so much for your invaluable feedback and constant encouragement. You guys are seriously the best cheerleaders ever! I wouldn't have had the guts to do this without you.

Thank you, **Steve**, for your suggestions, imagination, beautiful drawings, amazing cover design, and being the most perfect husband/best-friend/partner-in-crime ever. I love you too much!

About the Author

Rise of the Giants is Christine Marshall's debut novel. She is glad to finally be able to share this book with the world.

When Christine isn't typing away on her laptop, she probably has a book and a piece of chocolate in hand. She loves all kinds of books: YA fantasy, sci-fi, historical fiction, non-fiction, and even textbooks.

She also loves to play her ukulele, stand in the rain, and try new foods... but not all at the same time! Christine has moved over 20 times in the past 20 years, and firmly believes that people are more important than things.

Made in the USA
Columbia, SC
27 July 2023

20797435R00162